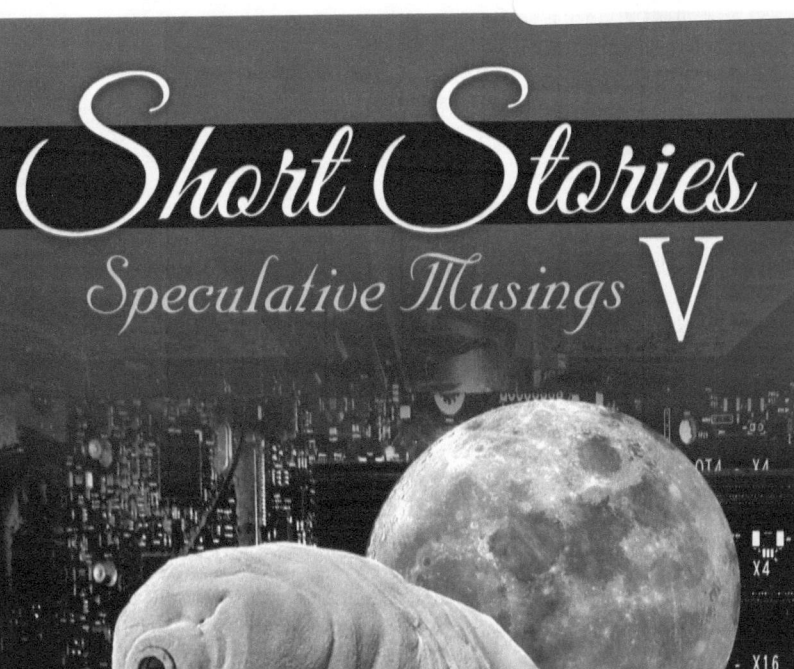

Short Stories
Speculative Musings V

RICH DiSILVIO

Author's Website: www.richdisilvio.com

- - - - - - - - - - - - - - - - -

Names: DiSilvio, Rich
Title: Short Stories V: Speculative Musings/ Rich DiSilvio
Description: New York, USA: DV Books, an imprint of Digital Vista, inc.
Identifiers: ISBN 978-1-950052-08-0 (paperback) |
ISBN 978-1-950052-07-3 (eBook)
Subjects: Short Stories | Speculative Fiction | Sci-Fi | Science Fiction | Suspense
Illustrations/Photos: 16

THE AUTHOR

Rich DiSilvio is an author of thrillers, mysteries, historical fiction and nonfiction. He has written books, historical articles, and commentaries for magazines and online resources. His passion for history, art, music, and architecture has yielded contributions in each discipline in his professional careers.

DiSilvio's work in the entertainment industry includes projects for historical documentaries, including James Cameron's *The Lost Tomb of Jesus, Killing Hitler, The War Zone* series, *Return to Kirkuk, Operation Valkyrie,* and cable TV shows and films such as *Tracey Ullman's State of the Union, Celebrity Mole, Blood Ties, Monty Python: Almost the Truth,* and many others.

He has written commentaries on the great composers (such as the top-rated Franz Liszt Site), and conceived and designed the Pantheon of Composers porcelain collection for the Metropolitan Opera, which also retailed throughout the USA and Europe.

His artwork and new media projects have graced the album covers and animated advertisements for numerous super-groups and celebrities, including, Pink Floyd, Yes, The Moody Blues, Cher, Madonna, Jay-Z, Willie Nelson, Miles Davis, the Rolling Stones, Alice Cooper, Queen, and many more.

As a software designer/developer, Rich pioneered the first interactive CD-ROM for educating staff and parents about Applied Behavioral Analysis (ABA) for training individuals with autism.

Rich lives in New York with his wife and has four children.

Contents

THE FACE OF EVIL

Iranian Imam Abdul Zarkarrah's bearded face twisted with animus as he spewed his venomous declaration on mainstream media. Instantaneously, Zarkarrah's speech ignited the airwaves like methane, as his virulent message struck fear into the hearts of millions. With pinched brows and piercing eyes, he spat, "In two hours time, the bogus state of Israel will be wiped off the map!"

Zarkarrah shifted heatedly at the podium as he stood before a large audience, dressed in his usual black aba and black turban, signifying his direct lineage to the Prophet Mohammad. Meanwhile, international news cameras zoomed in on his animated face, which instantaneously went viral on social media. "My predecessors have all spoken similar words, but *I*, Imam Abdul Zarkarrah, will make good on that promise, once and for all! The infidels of

Israel *will* feel my wrath, and *will* vanish in a nuclear flash!" Gazing skyward, he yelled, *"Allahu Akbar!"* to a cacophony of cheers.

Abdul's dead, black eyes then gazed deeply into each of the ten camera lenses, and simultaneously outward from millions of TV, computer, and cell phone screens across the globe, as his heated lips rustled his wiry beard with each new festered word, vile words that radiated the contempt and fanatical hatred that had long brewed in the hearts and minds of many Iranian leaders.

In the United States, the hour was 7:32 PM Eastern Standard Time, as President Carmen Alvarado Suarez gazed at the TV screen, while her skin rippled with goose bumps. Standing nearby, fourteen of her aides looked on with dread as the phone rang.

President Suarez's eyes remained glued to the TV screen as she reached over and picked up the phone.

"Yes?" She uttered anxiously.

On the line was Secretary of Defense Norman Bull. "Madame President, I'm sure you're watching the Imam as we speak..."

Carmen barely managed to mutter yes, as he stridently continued, "We *must* act swiftly, Madame President, time is of the essence. I propose we utilize our missiles in Turkey and send in ground troops immediately. I can mobilize in—"

"No!" President Suarez interrupted emphatically. "We will *not* jump into this without consulting the Israeli Prime Minister and our allies first. Is that understood?"

A disgruntled huff emanated out of the receiver. "Yeah, understood, Madame President. I await your orders."

"I need you here, Secretary, at the Oval Office. My staff is already here and I want you all close."

"Very well," he replied, and with that, Norman Bull abruptly hung up.

Carmen rolled her eyes. She and the hawkish Secretary never saw eye to eye. Meanwhile, the cell phones of her aides rang and soon a cacophony of voices reverberated off the walls of the Oval Office as they answered calls. Carmen's suit jacket was already showing signs of sweat, as Chief of Staff Marissa Levy said, "President Suarez, we need to know on which side of the fence Russia and China stand on this matter."

Suarez glanced at her and nodded firmly. "Yes, make the inquiries at once."

Meanwhile, 1,700 miles away, military engineer Lee Chan was sitting at his desk at Lockheed Martin in Littleton, Colorado, watching the harrowing telecast. As he gazed at the evil face on his flat screen TV, Lee's email alert sounded on his cell phone to the galloping melody of Rossini's *William Tell Overture*. He stood up, reached in his pocket, and gazed at the screen. It was his cousin, Hon Su, from China; a correspondence that both nations frowned upon due to the sensitive nature of their work and potential risks to national security.

China's ten-year-old prediction of becoming a superpower in 2025 to surpass the United States had finally reached fruition, and a draconian stranglehold on its innocent citizens had tightened with each succeeding year. With political and military relations strained, Lee was hesitant to even answer his cell phone, but Rossini's quicksilver tune only made his adrenaline surge and heart jump from a trot to a gallop, akin to Silver, the Lone Ranger's horse. Now sweaty with trembling hands, Lee blinked hard, then swiped up the *Receive Call* icon. "Hon! This is a *very* bad time. What is it?"

Hon Su's voice trembled. "Lee, you m-must help me escape this godforsaken country!"

Lee shook his head. "Hon, you must know that a war in the Middle East is about to erupt, perhaps igniting World War Three! Are you nuts?"

As Lee's eyes remained glued to the Imam's unsettling face on the TV screen, he nervously took the cell phone away from his ear. He was about to hang up, when he heard Hon's voice ring out: "Lee! *Please!* I have inside information about this telecast. Info that I *must* tell your president, *immediately!*"

Lee rolled his eyes and sighed as he returned the phone to his ear. "*What*, Hon? Don't toy with me!"

"I'm not!" Hon Su replied, breathing heavily and dead serious. "But I must tell her in person, so I need your help to book me a flight. I'm unable to buy a ticket. As you know, I'm prohibited from leaving the country." He caught his breath, and continued, "I'm already near the border and can make my way to Pokhara International Airport in Nepal in twenty minutes. Have a plane ticket ready for me there."

Lee glanced at the posters on the wall of the stealth fighters, drones, and ballistic missiles he designed, some pictured upon impact with their fiery discharges and mushroom clouds. He shook his head, often appalled at himself for falling into this destructive line of work. "Hon, Iran will bomb Israel in two hours. By the time you get here the war will have begun. And with nuclear weapons, it may be over by then, as well."

"Not so," Hon said confidently. "I'm telling you, I have inside info. Iran still hasn't managed to create nuclear weapons. They're lying. It will be a conventional campaign. We have time, but time *is* of the essence."

Lee plopped back down on his swivel chair and spun back and forth as he gritted his teeth. "Hon, even if that's true, how could I get you an audience with the President?"

"Lee, you're one of America's top military engineers. You have clout. And you have a cousin who is also a military engineer with valuable information that President Suarez must be made aware of, to avoid making a catastrophic mistake. I can prevent a nuclear face-off between America and Russia, but you *must* get me a plane ticket at Nepal's airport, and fast!"

"A faceoff with *Russia*?" Lee stopped swiveling. "What do *they* have to do with this?"

"Never mind, Lee, I'll tell you everything when we meet."

"If this is so critical, Hon, why can't you just tell me what it is you know to save time?"

"Because *my* life depends on it," Hon said, his voice racked with fear. "I hate to say this, Lee, but it's the only way to get you to buy me a ticket to freedom. If I told you, you'd leave me here to die. I have it on good authority that the Russians have learned that I'm privy to their covert operation and have already sent agents out to kill me. For God's sake, Lee, we're cousins, *family*...help me get out of this oppressive country and away from the Russians' hit men! *Please!*"

"Okay!" Lee conceded. "I'll buy you a ticket directly to Dulles Airport on a supersonic flight, which will cut your air time down to only five hours or so. Then I'll try to get through to the President to set up your meeting."

"You're the best!" Hon Su's grateful voice sounded. "I love you, Lee."

"And I you, Hon. I'll meet you in D.C. So, get your ass to Pokhara Airport right away. Be careful!"

Lee hung up, ordered the plane tickets, and put a call into Secretary of War Bill Hodges, whom he knew well. Lee didn't expect Bill to be able to put him through to the President, especially during a volatile crisis that was about to explode in two hours, but to his surprise, President Suarez's voice eventually came through the receiver: "Professor Chan, please make this quick!"

"Madame President, I'm flying my cousin clandestinely out of communist China. His name is Hon Su. He is also a military engineer and has vital information about the Imam's telecast. Information, he said, that can avert an all-out nuclear holocaust."

The President's dry lips furled. "Professor Chan, I am being inundated with time-sensitive calls that I must assess to make quick and intelligent decisions. I cannot wait around for your cousin to fly here from China, the war will have already commenced and God knows what state the Middle East and the world will be in at that late hour."

"I can tell you this much, Madame President, he said the Iranians are bluffing about their nuclear capability, this war will be waged with conventional weapons."

The President waved off her aides, who were all clamoring for her attention, and continued her phone conversation. "Thank you, Professor Chan, but we have that intel already. I'm in no hurry to push any nuclear buttons, but I can't say the same about Israel. So, this war *will* get ugly, very ugly. Therefore, containment and a quick end to this pending conflict is my goal. However, based upon your sterling reputation and the Secretary of War's recommendation, I will grant your meeting, even if it will be too late in the game. How soon can you and your cousin be here?"

"I booked him on a supersonic flight, President Suarez. He and I should arrive in six hours, around 1:30 AM, your time. Is that too late?"

The President laughed. "I already said you'd be too late, Professor."

As Lee got the joke—or perhaps it wasn't—she said, "I'll see you then." And the President hung up.

Five and a half hours later, Lee met Hon Su at Dulles Airport. The cousins hugged, but Lee swiftly eased him backward. "I imagine you heard the grim news on your flight; Israel fired two preemptive nuclear missiles before Iran even initiated the war. Tehran and Mashhad have been largely obliterated."

Hon Su's eyes widened in shock, having had no cellular service in flight, as Lee added with exasperation, "You said this wouldn't be a nuclear war, Hon! Now tell me, what the hell do you know!? If anything at all, you liar!"

With that, Lee grabbed Hon's elbow and walked him quickly toward his rented Prius, while Hon almost tripped.

Hon looked at Lee out of the corner of his eye. "Lee, I didn't lie. No one could have predicted that. I was referring to Iran's nuclear capabilities, not Israel's. My intel comes from my old college buddy, Jon Sing. You remember him; I spoke to you about him before, he's Manchurian, genuinely Chinese in *my* eyes, but unfortunately living in the Russian sector of Outer Manchuria."

As Lee nodded, Hon continued, "Well, Jon was the lead on one of Russia's top secret programs. Their intent was to surreptitiously start a war in the Middle East via deception, so they could consume their oil-rich territory. Therefore, they needed to make it look like the Iranians started it." As they entered the rented car, Hon quickly buckled his seatbelt, and added, "Their top secret project is called Clone Wolf."

Lee squinted as he pushed the electric ignition button. "Clone Wolf? What types of clones do they produce?"

As Lee hit the accelerator and began to drive, Hon replied. "You saw the evil result on TV, Lee, with millions of other duped viewers."

Lee almost hit a pedestrian, as he swerved and looked angrily at Hon. "Are you nuts! The Imam is a clone!? Get serious. There's *no way* the Russians mastered cloning, Hon." Lee abruptly pulled over and jammed on the brakes. As Hon's head almost went through the windshield, Lee spat, "I'm not going to look like a fool in front of the President with you telling an asinine tale like that! Biological cloning is *not* feasible, at least not yet!"

Hon steadied himself in the seat and looked at Lee sternly. "I never said a biological clone, you moron! The Imam you saw is a clone made from a variety of photos of the man, which were then put into a newly advanced 3D printer. The Russians mastered a process of emulating skin, hair, eyes, you name it, all of which look very real. The clone was then animated with servos and a voice recognition databank captured from Zarkarrah's many speeches. The Russians silently abducted Zarkarrah at night, so no one was aware he was missing. Then they setup a public broadcast early this morning. So, those who witnessed and videoed the Imam's warring hate speech in person gave further credence to it being authentic."

Lee's eyes veered left and right, deep in thought, then back at his cousin. His face mellowed. "I'm sorry for losing my head, Hon. I doubted you. I was wrong."

Hon reached over and patted his shoulder. "Don't worry, Lee. I forgive you. But I can never forgive those Russian pigs."

Lee nodded. "Yes, those sly bastards started a nuclear war."

A tear welled in Hon's eye. "Not only that. Those animals brutally murdered Jon Sing and his entire staff, then razed the laboratory to the ground to get rid of the evidence."

Lee took a deep breath and sighed. "Jesus Christ, this is a nightmare. We must tell the President, immediately!" He punched the accelerator and resumed driving, weaving through the streets of D.C. toward the White House.

Just then, a black SUV pulled up alongside them on the passenger's side. As the tinted window started to roll down, Lee eagerly looked over at the vehicle, then at Hon next to him. "Look at this, we have an escort."

A Glock emerged out of the SUV's window, as the stone-faced driver popped off two shots. The bullets shattered the windows of the Prius, sailing straight through and missing their intended targets. Lee swerved into the SUV, pushing the vehicle into the rear of a parked car. With a loud crash, the nose of the SUV crumbled like an accordion as the airbags inflated.

Meanwhile, Lee and Hon shivered with adrenaline as they sped away from the gunman, not knowing or caring if he survived the crash.

Some twenty minutes later, Lee and Hon found themselves being escorted into the Oval Office. As they entered the crowded room, packed with aides, the President looked up from the famous Resolute Desk. Heatedly, she pointed at the couch. "Have a seat, and make it quick!" she hissed. "I have a nuclear war on my hands—one that *you*, Professor Chan, said would be conventional!"

Lee swallowed hard, still rattled by his near-death encounter, as he replied sternly, "President Suarez, *nothing* about this mess is conventional. We were just attacked by a hit man on our way here, who appeared to be one of your SS men. So what exactly *is* going on?"

The President didn't like Lee's tone, but was mystified herself about the intended hit job, as her eyes veered at the Director of Home Land Security, who then looked at the Director of the FBI, who in turn looked at the Director of the CIA. Each shook their heads firmly in the negative and shrugged, bewildered. She looked back at Lee and Hon. "I assure you, I authorized no such hit, Professor. Neither did my security team. After all, why on Earth would we want either of you harmed or killed?"

"That's the ten thousand dollar question, isn't it," Lee replied curtly as he nervously rubbed his sweaty head.

Meanwhile, Hon jumped into the conversation. "Madame President, I have fled China to save my life. The hit man most likely was a Russian assassin."

"And why is that?"

"Because of what I know." As Hon relayed the astonishing news about the Imam clone, the President and her aides rolled their eyes. The story was simply too absurd to believe. But as Hon expounded upon the wild tale, offering viable explanations and key names, some of whom the security staff acknowledged as known Russian operatives, it began to gel. The Russian's dastardly scheme to start a war, with the intention of moving in with ground troops and conventional weapons to eventually seize the entire Middle East, made perfect sense. Especially since the Russians and Chinese had already sent troops into the Middle East over the past three hours. As such, the dark and deadly picture came to light; the effective broadcast of a life-like clone of Abdul Zarkarrah inciting war was a vile cinematic ploy, one executed with even greater expertise than a Hollywood studio.

The President leaned back in her chair as her shoulders slouched. Under heated breath, she uttered, "Those barbarians! I thought I was making progress with them when they agreed to side with us in this damn war. But it's all been a ruse."

Secretary of Defense Norman Bull looked at her and huffed. "I told you we should have sent troops in right away. Now the Russians already have an edge and will consume the entire Middle East, like they did Eastern Europe last year."

The President smirked as she glared at Norman, never liking the man personally or politically, but now annoyed that she should have heeded his advice. "We need more than a presence on the ground or drone strikes, Secretary Bull," she said. "We need to bring this Russian charade to light, so the world knows they started this war. I have managed to get the Israelis to refrain from using more nuclear weapons, but even though we've momentarily diverted an all-out nuclear war, we have the entire Muslim world united and fully engaged, all trying to wipe Israel off the map."

Meanwhile, Secretary of War Bill Hodges opined, "I think we should confront the damn Russians head on! They've interfered with our elections, re-seized their satellite nations throughout Eastern Europe, and now want to swallow up the Middle East for their oil. Even though they claim to be on our side fighting the United Islamic Coalition, we now know their true intent. Let's cripple the bastards!"

President Suarez sat upright and snapped, "And just how do you propose we do that without igniting World War Three!?"

"By covertly crippling them in the field, Madame President. We outfit our troops in UIC uniforms and planes and push them damn Russkies right out of the Fertile Crescent."

The president shook her head and snickered. "Jesus Christ! You must be kidding? You want us to stoop to their barbaric level of deceit? That will never happen on my watch, Bill!"

She glanced around the room at all her aides. "Speak up! I want to hear viable solutions."

An uneasy silence pervaded the room, until Hon Su spoke up. "Excuse me, Madame President, but, as you said, I think an immediate and all-out campaign to broadcast the Russians' devious plan would be in your best interest. That would cause Israel *and* the UIC to unite against the Russians and do the dirty work for you."

As everyone in the room contemplated Hon Su's words, most nodded, as the Secretary of the Treasury said, "He has a valid point, President Suarez. Why should we get dragged into this mess? It would cost us millions of dollars, thousands of lives, and ignite a World War if we confront Russia with military might, openly or clandestinely."

As many echoed those words, the President looked at Hon Su, then at the Director of the CIA, Sarah Chambers. "Sarah, how can we verify that Hon Su's story about the Russian's cloning scheme is true?"

Sarah touched her earpiece. "I have people looking in to it as we speak, Madame President. They've been on top of this for the past hour, ever since Hon Su arrived and brought this to our attention."

Hon Su's eyes nervously glanced around the room, uncomfortable in seeing a sea of suspicious eyes all fixated on him. "What I told you *is* the truth," he said defensively. "As I told you, the Russians killed my friend, Jon Sing, his entire staff, *and* obliterated the entire plant to conceal their guilt. So you won't find hard evidence, but I'm telling you now, if you don't reveal their crime to the world community, this war *will* end with Russia consuming the entire Middle East and its oil." As all eyes remained glued on Hon Su, he continued, "America's long-held fears of the spread of communism will reach unprecedented heights if you dither! Just like how you and your allies hesitated with Hitler, allowing him to consume one nation after another. By the time he invaded Poland it was too late. You missed your wake-up call back then, and you're about to miss it once again. You *will* regret your inaction." With added emphasis, he added, "Mark my words!"

As minds began to change, the Secretary of the Treasury stepped forward. "I agree. We must put the blame where it belongs, *at once,* to change the course of this war in our favor."

Chief of Staff Marissa Levy, chimed in, "I, too, agree, Madame President. I can get a media campaign started immediately, with your permission."

Secretary of War Bill Hodges shook his head and huffed. "I, for one, don't think we should move on this just on the word of one man—a Chinese man from communist China, no less. A country that, like Russia, has engaged in hegemony and is hellbent on technologically and economically bringing us to our knees."

Lee Chan had been standing quietly by a portrait of Thomas Jefferson, but now stepped forward, and retorted, "Listen! My cousin has been at the forefront of China's technological revolution and holds an eminent position there, as much as I do here." His eyes scanned the assemblage. "Except for one major difference; he fled his nation to come here to alert us and seek asylum. He is *not* a communist!" Lee looked at Secretary Hodges, "I've known you for many years, Bill, but I must say, I find your remarks quite racist!"

Bill rolled his eyes. "Save your race card for the track, Lee," he said wittily to a round of stifled smiles. "Speaking the truth doesn't mean someone is racist. We all know that not all Chinese people are corrupt or hostile. In fact, I, and most Americans, know that the greater population isn't; they're unfortunate prisoners in a ruthless regime. It's the tyrannical leaders in China who are not honorable or our allies, Lee. They have an agenda, one that seeks world domination. Yet, unlike impatient America, China has been on the slow and steady track. They have a long-term philosophy that is counter to ours, but nonetheless, they *will* cause global mayhem if not checked."

Hon Su finally interjected, "China has no interest in the Middle East, Mr. Secretary. It's the Russians who have been consuming nations."

"Oh, no interest, you say," Bill retorted. "So why were Chinese troops swiftly deployed in the Middle East, even before the Russians had boots on the ground?"

President Suarez slapped her desk. "I heard enough!" She looked at her Chief of Staff. "Marissa, move forward with the media campaign, immediately. The Russians have meddled in our government for years and have now meddled in the Middle East, this time with a truly despicable act. Bad enough we had to deal with fake videos, but this cloning of world leaders has taken it too far! We now have a war on our hands; millions have already been incinerated in Iran with two nuclear blasts, while thousands are fighting as we speak in Iran, Iraq, Syria, Jordan, Israel and many other nations. This must stop!" She pointed to the door. "Go, Marissa. Make this happen!"

As Marissa scurried out the door, several aides shook their heads, while others felt the action was not only proper, but overdue.

As Lee Chan and Hon Su breathed sighs of relief, the President asked that all in attendance remain in the Oval Office until further notice. She knew that once the media blitz commenced and went viral she would need to assess the situation quickly, and having her staff at her fingertips was critical.

As the assemblage made themselves somewhat comfortable, sitting on couches and chairs to deliberate further, Lee Chan looked at his cousin and smiled. "Hon, I'm glad I was able to assist you in fleeing China. Your input has been critical and saved the U.S. from making a terrible mistake."

Hon Su smiled and patted Lee's back. "Yes, that's why I had to get here as fast as I could. Once the truth hits the airwaves, this war will turn everyone against Russia and finally stop them in their tracks."

An hour passed as refreshments and appetizers were served. Meanwhile, Lee and Hon kept busy by looking at the historic memorabilia in the Oval Office, including the portrait of Eleanor Roosevelt that the new president had personally mounted on the wall herself. Moments later, the president cleared her throat and directed everyone's attention to the large flat screen TV, hanging on the wall. "I just received word," she said. "The first of many broadcasts will go live in two minutes."

As the gathering looked up at the screen, the news commentator prepared the audience for the upcoming breaking news. The Oval Office was silent, as each official gazed at the TV in anticipation. Then the moment arrived, when the news anchor's image cut to a video sequence, featuring the notorious clips of the Abdul Zarkarrah's evil face as it contorted with venom. The video collage then segued to a CGI dramatization of how the Russian cloning process most likely operated. As some aides smiled others cringed.

Meanwhile, almost everyone's cell phone began ringing. As each answered their calls from domestic and international contacts, the president looked on anxiously, awaiting their feedback. Soon, aides began relaying the responses from their contacts and from world news organizations, which were spreading the shocking revelation. Russian diplomats flooded the phones of international ambassadors, pleading innocence, while generals of all nations engaged on the battlefield were stymied, unsure of what remedial actions should be taken.

The Oval Office was a chaotic discord of voices, each trying to inform the president of the latest developments, when the Director of the CIA bellowed, "Can I have everyone's attention! *Please!*"

As they all stopped and looked her way, Sarah glanced irritably around the room, her teeth clenched tight with animus and her finger pressed to her earpiece. "I just received word that the SUV involved in trying to assassinate Hon Su, and possibly Professor Chan, was located. The assassin survived the crash and is now in custody." She scanned the room, seeking Hon Su, but couldn't locate him among the shifting bodies. "The hit man was in fact Russian," she continued. "However, he was not trying to kill Hon Su for leaking information about their Clone Wolf program, because…" she paused, then added, "They never had such a program. It was Hon Su's lab in China that developed the clone!"

As everyone gasped, Sarah went on, "We have several trusted sources corroborating this as I speak." Sarah pressed her earpiece tighter to her ear, trying to listen to the breaking news, then continued, "What we now know is this... It was a Chinese stratagem: First, to use the clone of Imam Zarkarrah to ignite a war between Iran and Israel; then have their operative, Hon Su, implicate the Russians as the culprits. That, in turn, would incite a multi-national bloodbath that would annihilate themselves and allow China to walk in and take the prize—*oil*, to keep their growing machine well lubricated and burning at an exponential pace."

Secretary of War Bill Hodges spat, "Damn them! I knew it was the Chinese!"

Meanwhile, everyone in the room turned in different directions, looking for Hon Su, including Lee Chan, who perplexingly spun around, equally baffled.

President Suarez stood up and blasted, "Where the hell did Hon Su go!?" A refrain echoed by many.

As the gathering gazed at Lee Chan and stepped aggressively toward him, Lee cowered and pleaded, "I'm innocent, I swear! I, too, was duped. I don't know where he went. He was here a minute ago." His head spun around like an owl's, nervously hoping to spot his wily cousin, but had no such luck.

Meanwhile, Bill Hodges dashed out the door, as Secretary of Defense Bull said, "Hon Su can't get too far, we'll catch the bastard."

Meanwhile, President Suarez's misleading newscast caused widespread mayhem among nations as Israeli and UIC troops fired upon Russian soldiers on the battlefield, inciting Russia to retaliate with nuclear force. The Middle East illuminated into a fiery caldron of utter destruction and insanity. Meanwhile, Chinese troops had retreated to the Chinese border wearing radioactive gear, waiting for the carnage to mount and the dust to settle to signal their conquest.

Radio dispatches were immediately sent out to generals, alerting them to the mistaken broadcast, while diplomats and NATO officials bickered and tried to ascertain the *real* truth.

To everyone in the Oval Office's dismay, word was received that Hon Su somehow managed to escape.

President Suarez's face fell into the palms of her hands as she slouched over the Resolute Desk, no longer resolute as she seethed in a vortex of gloom.

EXTINCTION

I recall fifty years ago reading in a 2020 edition of *Discover* magazine how a million species were in danger of extinction. Why such critical news was not relentlessly plastered on every TV screen and across all social media platforms still baffles me, but ignore the warning signs humankind did.

Obviously, Earth's natural course of evolution was partly responsible, but humankind's wanton abuse and arrogant neglect held the largest pie-chart slice of blame.

Big business polluted the planet in every conceivable way, from their industrial plants defiling the air with toxic pollution or chemical spillages contaminating water reservoirs, to their waste products filling the oceans with plastic bottles and bags, which wiped out scores of aquatic species, as well as birds and reptiles. Added to the septic surge was the awakening of China to the modern advances of the Western world, thereby almost doubling the doses of toxins at a dizzying pace that exponentially swept across the planet like the Black Death, wiping out not just animal life, but also bringing humankind to the brink of annihilation.

The extinction of a million animals was not contained to only those most people imagined, as the loss of insects—vital to pollinating plants and essential for human nutrition or for the manufacturing of critical medicines—proved equally devastating, as was the loss of the plants themselves. Along with the diminishing of essential vegetation were the deaths of vital tropical rainforests and the deforesting of millions of acres of trees for wood and paper products. In essence, the highly touted brilliance and bold innovations of humankind had caused the destruction of scores of various life forms on Earth and eventually the breakdown and ultimate demise of Earth itself.

While a morose aura of gloom beclouds this critique of human folly—and burdens my soul with these bitter words, which rightfully bludgeon our stupidity—fear not. For amid the ominous blanket of death and destruction a silver lining had eked its way out of the blackness and prevailed.

Oddly enough, in that same 2020 *Discover* magazine, another interesting article appeared; namely, *Brains Brought Back to Life*. Now, while that breakthrough received scant attention, due to limited success working on pigs' brains, researchers in the shadows continued their quest to rejuvenate pig and monkey brains that were clinically deemed *dead*. Fortunately, over the next ten years, scientists had advanced to experimenting with human brains, and I was one such lucky candidate. For there were only two other successful human brain experiments, that of a young, brilliant astrophysicist, named Olivia Sanchez, and Albert Einstein, which fortunately humankind had the good sense to preserve his brain. Being resurrected, at least in mind only, Einstein had been put to the task of helping the brightest among us to save humankind and our beloved planet from extinction.

To clarify the selection process of this miraculous brain rejuvenation procedure, I must make clear that the global crisis took precedence in their decisions, and amid much debate and fierce protests, only the brains of people who could help solve the grave problems were selected. You see, Olivia and I had been Nobel Prize winners for scientific discoveries, yet oddly enough had been the victims of untimely deaths; Olivia's by cancer at age twenty-eight, and mine…well, mine was by murder. I was the victim of a gruesome home invasion.

My wife Barbara and I were in bed, when I heard the jarring sound of broken glass downstairs. I turned on the nightlight and told Barbara to stay put, while I investigated. Amid the dim glow of light, I slipped on my pajamas and walked slowly down the steps. I turned on the living room light and crept quietly through, scanning each window. All was clear, so I advanced into the kitchen. Again, my eyes scanned the windows, and again, all was clear. No broken glass to be seen. I was naturally baffled and quite nervous. I then entered the den, only to hear a terrible shriek! I couldn't mistake Barbara's heart-wrenching scream.

I turned and dashed up the stairs, only to see the most horrifying sight; Barbara's body lay butchered on the bed, our white satin sheets stained with crimson remnants of her liquid life force. I was paralyzed with shock, until I heard footsteps behind me! That's when I turned to see the visage of my own death, as a ghastly figure emerged out of the darkness; his face twisted with psychotic wrath, while his two crazed eyes peered right into my soul, like rapiers, slicing and slashing away the precious essence that once constituted my life. Within seconds, thirty-two years of my life had been erased, as the pain of the assailant's bloody slashes had yielded only blackness, no pain, no thoughts, no heartbeat, *nothing*—I, James Watterson, was dead.

But, as I said, there is a silver lining, and a very luminous one indeed. While I was officially declared dead by the powers that be, such was not the consensus of the research scientists at Cognition Re-Ignition Enterprises.

Oren Hatfield, lead scientist, spearheaded the Jumpstart Program that yielded the successful rejuvenations of three dead brains; in this case mine. And while that was many years ago, other advances had emerged out of the dying planet, as a small group of engineers and scientists, which included Olivia, had also developed great strides in aeronautics and space exploration. That was achieved through national space agencies and private enterprises.

So, while the Earth crumbled and perished under immense stress, caused by human indulgences, human ingenuity enabled fifteen percent of humanity to escape the catastrophe and head out into deep space. Utilizing Mars as the first rest stop on the journey, then Saturn's moon, Enceladus, our travels took us across the solar system and out into the Milky Way, where exoplanet Z-15 was discovered to be inhabitable. While it's no comparison to the once beautiful and magnificent planet Earth, Z-15 has proven to be an exemplary environment for fostering Earth species of plants and animals and the new breed of humans who now inhabit this planet.

The selection process for Operation Salvation was extremely stringent, and while opposition and even hostile attempts to sabotage the mission were encountered, the selection of only those deemed "productive and compatible" were chosen. While even I had objections to some of the subjective requirements, overall, Operation Salvation proved to be a major success.

All life-forms on planet Z-15 are abundant and are engineered to maintain equilibrium, education is first-rate, crime is in single digits, food sources and manufacturing are plentiful and environmentally safe, and conservation takes a high priority among the leaders. Ten leaders are elected every two years, with no one individual being able to serve more than two terms. Meanwhile, voters only consist of those who obtain a Sublime Degree in Intelligence (SDI). This is not solely based on academics, but of equal importance, common sense and practical experience in real world situations. For it had been clearly proven that not all those who had gone to college and flaunted paper certificates and high IQs were capable of making wise decisions. Creative thinking often comes from the least likely of places, such as the examples of Henry Ford and Thomas Edison, neither genius having formal educations.

Naturally, all elected leaders must likewise hold a SDI, as no leader could possibly serve the greater good without a solid combination of knowledge, practical experience, and common sense; something the vast majority of politicians in the past lacked. Additionally, the ill effects of religious intolerance and hatred have been eradicated. Therefore, the extinction of a large share of human life that had been unproductive, incompatible, or hostile—due to the archaic aspects of religious dogma and draconian politics— had proven to be the ultimate solution to the woes of humanity. Perfection has finally been achieved. Perhaps the words of John Lennon said it best—*Imagine!*

†††

Oren Hatfield looked at the monitor, as the brain waves of James Watterson oscillated and digital voice software reproduced his dictation of human events. Oren turned off the audio system, then looked at Donna Lee, his associate. Glumly, he said, "Oddly enough, just being a brain in a large Petri dish, that's all James can do; *imagine*."

Donna's grieved face couldn't conceal the horror of the dead world in which they lived, as the Earth was in total breakdown, rapidly deteriorating as floods devastated the land, wild fires burned out the last patches of tropical rain forests, and the eroded ozone layer intensified the Sun's devastating gamma rays, killing the last remnants of life on the planet.

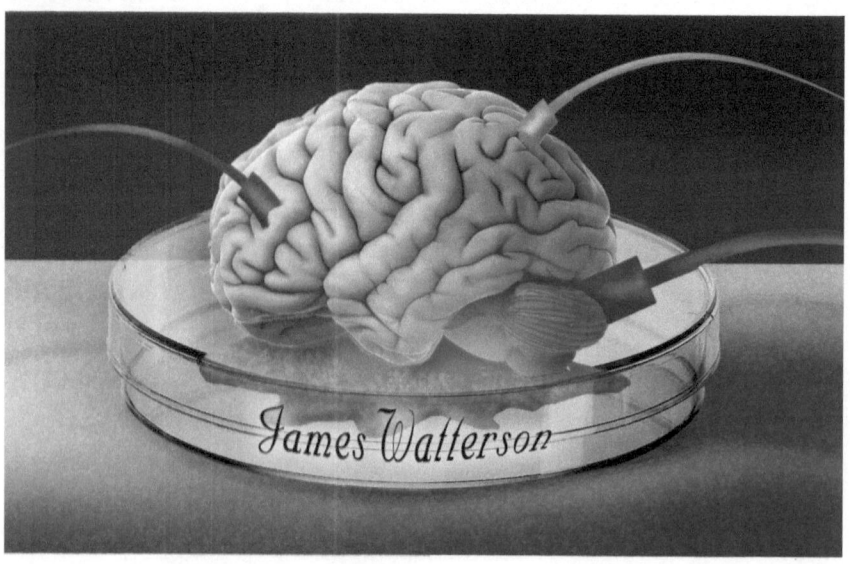

Donna wiped the tear that broke free as an Earthquake rattled the laboratory. Steadying herself, she looked back down at James' brain wriggling in the Petri dish. "He's lived without a body for forty years, blind and unable to feel the loving touch of a fellow human. He's just a globular organ pulsing with nutrients and electrical charges that we use to keep him cognizant. He has no idea that we never managed to leave Earth. All those lies we told him, to give him hope, were futile." She looked back up at Oren. "Were *we* the monsters?"

Hatfield's head fell as he sighed. "It doesn't matter anymore," he uttered, as he gazed out the window at the ominous holocaust, which was seconds away from annihilating the entire planet. "We tried to save our race and this planet, but failed. We did our best." He peered over at the Petri dish of Olivia's brain, which had been disconnected from life support moments ago, then at Einstein's brain, which, due to aging, had struggled to maintain itself and had likewise been disconnected months ago. "Even Einstein's brain proved useless," he said. "I thought he could have helped us to devise a solution to escape extinction. Even NASA and all the global space organizations couldn't manage to cultivate another planet successfully. We humans brought this upon ourselves. We were reckless and arrogant."

With a thunderous clash, the entire building started to collapse. Terrified, Oren and Donna embraced each other as tears rolled down their cheeks, the last tears ever shed by the human species. Large steel beams and asphalt-roofing materials rained down, crushing them both into pulp; the human race had finally reached its ultimate destination—extinction.

Another earthquake, more intense, tore apart the planet's crust, while fires incinerated cities and floods eroded coastlines. The Earth's surface was savagely mangled and transformed, as the continents diminished in size and shape, while Australia and Antarctica no longer existed, having turned into large sandbars sitting miles below the ocean's rising surface. Every island on the planet sat at the bottom of the sprawling sea, a sea vacant of life. All was lost, as the Earth became a barren wasteland with windswept dunes and empty rolling seas, as only the sounds of waves washing ashore rippled the still, dead air.

†††

Six million years later, three eight-legged travelers landed on Earth, the species hailing from the planet's nearby orbiting satellite. The evolved mutations had been the result of Tardigrade microorganisms that had crash-landed on the moon during Israel's failed Beresheet Lunar mission in 2018. The extremely hearty Tardigrades had developed into large-scale organisms, able to survive harsh lunar temperatures, even with limited oxygen. Over the next two thousand years, the Tardigrades colonized Earth and life thrived once again.

Along with the Tardigrades came other microbes and bacteria, blossoming into a lush ecosystem of large and small life forms, the Tardigrades being the ultimate masters, perched at the top of the food chain and standing ten feet tall. The mighty microbes—with their armored exteriors, large claws, and no eyes—had finally prevailed and ruled over planet Earth, thanks to the human species' fundamental flaw—ignorance, the foolish belief that they were the brilliant masters of the universe.

The extinction of the smartest and deadliest species had yielded to the rise of the most overlooked and underrated species on the planet, a species unseen by the human eye, yet so vigorous, resilient, and critical to the creation and maintenance of *all* life-forms, that their superior genetic code, programmed for survival, should have never been trivialized. With their long-lost planet now reclaimed, the new paradigm was complete—Earth belonged to the Tardigrades and their microbial minions. For them, extinction was *not* an option.

TALES OF THE HEART

My body quivers to the soft gentle touch of her hand as it smears gel over my bare chest. Amid the room's darkness I can barely see Susan's striking silhouette as her hand continues to roam around my rib cage, then up toward my pectorals. Suddenly, my heart flutters and almost causes me to chuckle, as the sensation of the cold, gooey liquid titillates my senses.

Under different circumstances, this could be the prelude to an erotic interlude. However, this is no romantic escapade or anything remotely humorous. Susan Bower is a young and pretty lab technician performing an echocardiogram on my troubled heart. Diagnosed two years ago with severe Atrial Fibrillation, I have been through a battery of tests and even two ghastly operations. The first of which I was told would be 99% successful. Either they lied or I'm one unlucky SOB.

The ablation required sending a catheter up through the vein in my thigh, right into the pulsing chambers of my heart. Then, essentially, they electrocuted my heart to activate the erratic heartbeat so they could map and locate the nerves that were misfiring and causing the fibrillation. This, mind you, was all done with the patient, *me*, wide-awake! After two hours of being electrocuted and sent into near-fainting arrhythmias, the heart's malignant nerves were digitally located and marked. I was then put under general anesthesia to ablate, or burn, the aberrant culprits. Well, despite their efforts, or the destruction of my heart cells, and their bogus claim of a 99% success rate, here I am, once again, getting my heart monitored. And that's even after my second operation entailed the installation of a pacemaker, which hasn't remedied the situation.

As Susan's pretty face glows, not from any amorous affair, but rather from her computer screen, she captures all the data, clicks "Test Complete", then turns on the harsh LED lights in the room.

As I squint and my pupils dilate to the bright light, she places a small wad of paper towels on my chest. "There you go, Mr. Davis. If you need more, let me know?"

I sit upright and wipe the goo off my chest and say, "I guess there were no miraculous changes, huh?"

She spins around and looks at me with genuinely sad eyes. "I'm not supposed to say, Mr. Davis. I'm only the lab tech." Her eyes peer back toward the door, ensuring no one's in sight, then whispers, "But, I'm afraid not. I'm so sorry."

As I button up my shirt, she adds, "Has Dr. Goldberg's prognosis changed?"

My eyes peer up at Susan's young face, reminding me of my own vibrant youth. As if a deer in headlights, my mind drifts into a dreamy haze, as distant visions of Eileen, the love of my life, flow into my head: The woman who made my once healthy heart flutter with passion, a passion I had never known before or since, as I can still vividly recall our fateful meeting that day, back in 1989. Oddly enough, it was an optimistic time, when even the Berlin Wall was finally being bulldozed and battered by the hands of thousands of East and West Germans, euphoric in the notion of being reunited once again and free of the tyrannical shackles of communism. My heart, too, felt liberated, jubilant, and fervently united with another's heart, beating as one. It was a landmark moment, a phenomenal love, perhaps even a blinding infatuation that drew me to this fireball of life, vitality, wit, and wholesome beauty. Eileen was like no other woman I had ever encountered, she was my Venus de Milo, tenfold.

No stranger to romance, I had dated many women in my twenty-four years on Earth prior to meeting Eileen, but none, *none*, ever aroused every fiber of my being like her. It was as if I were sleepwalking through life until that fateful day, the day I knew this woman had to be my wife. Our cognitive sparks and animal magnetism collided, like a neutron bullet causing a fission reaction, making our union a volatile fireball of nuclear energy, a blinding radiance that anyone in our vicinity couldn't help but notice, as our luminous lives even intensified and enlivened those around us.

Our wedding celebration was a marvel in every sense, but that was just the beginning. As the years rolled by, Eileen and I had two beautiful children, each with a unique stamp of originality, and each with tender hearts beating to a genetic blueprint conjured by the fiery love of their two parents. Unfortunately, not all human creations are born under such euphoric circumstances, but when true love is the catalyst, the creation of life is one of the most profound, mystifying, and beautiful moments in all of human existence. That miniscule sperm cells and eggs can create an amphibian-like being within the womb, encased in fluid, and perform what took human evolution millions of years to do—from our aquatic ancestors to our current, land-dwelling state—in the matter of only nine months, is beyond doubt miraculous!

Soon, days turned into months, and months into years. The joy of rearing our precious children consumed us both, as Eileen and I poured our hearts and souls into every waking moment of their lives. The tender memories of the many family escapades we shared still fills my heart with sheer bliss, moments of their first words, first walking steps, first time riding a bike, or swimming, or skiing, or playing soccer, and the time spent studying with them until they flew off, heading to college and starting a life of their own. The grand journey was the thrill of my life, a journey that included my own ventures into nanotechnology, where I pioneered the first micro-robotic cell to travel in the bloodstream to fight and eradicate cancer. It was a discovery long sought after by tens of thousands of scientists since the beginning of recorded history, dating back many millennia.

In hindsight, perhaps if I expended my time finding a cure for heart disease my fate would be different, but I now awaken out of my foray to see the cold and barren examination room, as Susan stands before me, awaiting my response to her question; namely, "Has Dr. Goldberg's prognosis changed?"

I look at Susan and shake my head. "I'm afraid not. He gives me a month, at best." As I hop off the examination table, I continue, "But who am I to complain? I've lived a fairly long and happy life, one that will even save countless patients from the ravages of cancer." As she forces out a smile from her empathetic, young face, I add, "You have all of your life ahead of you, Susan. Enjoy every moment, and make every moment count, because it goes fast. Sometimes *too* fast!"

Unexpectedly, my heart twists with pain, weeping with sorrow, as I find myself unable to ward off the grim reality before me. Wearing a pseudo smile to offer strength to the living, I walk out the door and into the dark and surreal realm of a dead future, one that will erase all of my precious heartfelt memories forever…unless, of course, the ancient myth about God reveals itself to be true.

My scientific mind says *not so*, but my tender heart says *yes*. The truth awaits me soon enough, as I grab my aching heart, stumble, and fall to the ground. Lying on my back, I clutch my stuttering heart and gaze skyward, my eyes playing tricks on me, as I enter a nebulous cloud of…

PROXIMA B

Billions looked on with horror as a massive meteorite crashed into the moon. Instantly, the night sky ignited with a fiery flash of silent light. As many gasped, others hugged their children and wept. Moments later, the ominous shockwave arrived. Windows shattered and buildings vibrated as the wall of sound thundered across the globe, feeling as if the planet were jolted out of its orbit.

Astroengineer Robert Fermi, descendent of the famous physicist Enrico Fermi, had been monitoring the meteorite for well over a year, so the catastrophic fireball that lit the night sky and its blistering shockwave came as no surprise. He well knew its origin.

Pulsar X-17 was the result of a supernova. Upon implosion, massive chunks of debris escaped the blast and barreled through the Milky Way, with one large meteorite speeding furiously toward Earth's solar system.

Fermi and his peers had worriedly been calculating the huge meteorite's trajectory with the hopes that it would bypass Earth. However, they soon realized that DOW—or *Day Of Wrath*, as the meteorite was called—was on a crash course with Earth. As DOW approached at blinding speed, it met with a timely obstruction, crashing into the moon with devastating force, while Earth was spared its day of wrath. Or so they thought.

The new distorted shape of the moon was a chilling sight. Most people gazed up at the disfigured satellite with dread, while the romantics looked on with heavy hearts, the vision of moonstruck lovers now forever defiled. Meanwhile, Apple Computers was quick to exploit the catastrophe for publicity by stating that the moon now looked like their logo—an apple with a bite mark.

However, Fermi and his team were not romantics, nor money mongers seeking to cash in on a catastrophe, and were now scrambling to devise a plan for the very survival of Earth itself. What soon became apparent was that the moon's orbital path had been altered by the collision, and the latest calculations confirmed Fermi's fears; the moon had swerved off course and would eventually collide into Earth.

As everyone knew, no fortuitous intervention or space anomaly could save Earth now. The clock had started, giving Earthlings two years at most to either divert the crippled moon's trajectory or abandon Earth. While several world leaders suggested firing nuclear warheads to divert the moon's path, many scientists speculated that the blasts would create massive debris that would inevitably veer toward Earth and cause comparable destruction.

Meanwhile, Fermi had anticipated the Earth being obliterated by the rogue meteorite over a year ago and had received funding to build a new spaceship. Outfitted with all the latest technologies the twenty-fifth century had to offer, the AstralArk-1, as Fermi called it, was a marvel of ingenuity. However, despite the craft's impressive speed, Fermi was stymied, he knew it was still insufficient to make the long trek in a practical timeframe. Its destination happened to be Proxima b, an exoplanet with a habitable atmosphere that orbited around the red dwarf star Proxima Centauri, the closest star to Earth. However, *closest*, in space terms meant 4.24 light years away. And while nanocrafts had been sent there with lasers two centuries ago, the missions were halted when wars, economic slumps, and pandemics depleted funding and crippled space explorations.

Sitting at his computerized desk at NASA, Fermi was lost in thought, gazing at the schematics of his spaceship's engines, when Juan Farjitas, his twenty-seven-year-old secretary, buoyantly entered his office. With a luminous grin, Juan approached him. "Professor, your ship has been tested and passed with flying colors!"

Fermi looked up and nodded with a half-smile. "That's swell, Juan. But, as you know, it will never reach Proxima b in our lifetime, unless I can devise a way to increase its velocity. While the use of lasers to propel nanocrafts at one-fifth the speed of light has been used for two hindered years, no new propulsion system has been devised for large-scale spacecraft. And I've only hit one dead end after another. It doesn't look promising."

Juan's smile dissipated. He thought for sure Fermi, the savant of their age, would have worked out a solution by now. The reality that they only had two years to come up with a solution struck him hard once again. It was a thought he preferred to avoid by digging deep into his work. "I hate to be a pessimist, Professor, but you said AstralArk would take ninety-three years to reach Proxima b. So, no one will survive that trip, unless you, well..." Juan didn't care to reiterate what the Professor already knew, and he changed gears. "I guess we have to look at the bright side, Professor, at least the four hundred passengers on your ship will have a slim chance of finding another habitable planet along their travels."

Fermi looked at Juan with little enthusiasm. "The odds of that is practically zero, Juan. Proxima b is the only known exoplanet close to Earth capable of sustaining life. We've sent countless nanoprobes there and elsewhere over the past two centuries. And even if by some miracle the crew could find another planet, that means I can only save four hundred people...correction, two hundred people, since they'll have to carry livestock and a variety of plant and animal species to populate the new world."

Fermi paused as the bleak reality of his mission sunk in deeper, despite knowing his efforts would indeed save a mere few. He looked up a Juan, knowing he was looking at a dead young man who wouldn't make the cut. His heart twisted with each thought of those he couldn't save, but it was time to at least enlighten Juan to the flight plan, that much he owed him.

"Juan, there *will* be a handful of survivors. You see, a hundred and fifty of the two hundred passengers who board the ship will be female infants. Once they reach their mid thirties, they will be artificially inseminated to give birth to children who will live long enough to survive the journey, since the majority of other passengers will age out and die. But this only saves a handful of human beings, Juan. The billions of lives that will die here on Earth, once the moon crashes into us, gives me no rest."

Juan swallowed hard. The AstralArk-1 may have been larger than Noah's Ark, but the reality that he and billions of others would be obliterated by a collision with the moon was not only terrifying but also psychologically and spiritually devastating. He wondered why God, if in fact He does exist, would condemn Earth once again to such a violent and horrible fate.

As he noticed Fermi gaze down at his digital blueprints, Juan discreetly pivoted sideways, reached into his breast pocket and pulled out a flask filled with straight tequila. Quickly, he snuck a swig. As he put it back and spun around, Fermi looked up and nodded. "It's all right, Juan. That normally would never be tolerated, but under these dire circumstances, I get it. But as for me, I can't cloud my mind, not at this critical juncture of our planet's very existence. I must find a solution, somehow."

The news blaring on the televised hologram, some twelve feet away, didn't help matters, as the commentator spoke of the panic and pandemonium that was breaking out worldwide. The fear of Earth's untimely demise caused millions to quit their jobs and revel in wanton and criminal behavior. In essence, they were breaking the chains of government and religion and just trying to live it up, however they saw fit. 3D-images of people engaging in looting, lust, and mindless mayhem filled the hologram projection. Riots, shootings, burnings, rapes, and all sorts of bedlam marred every nation across the doomed globe.

Fermi irritably switched off the digital implant behind his ear, which wirelessly transmitted his synaptic thoughts and drafting capabilities to the large computer screen that comprised the entire top of his desk. With a huff, he gazed up at the hologram once again and rubbed his weary eyes, nauseated by the downfall of civilization right before his eyes. He gazed back at Juan. "Perhaps that's why Noah was given a chance to start anew. Without guidance or hope most people become animals."

Juan just stared at the hologram projection through his tequila-tainted eyes, grief-stricken, and unable to offer a rebuttal.

Two days later, NASA engineer Kristen Lindsey came running into Fermi's office, panic-stricken. "Excuse me, Professor!" she gasped, trying to catch her breath. "Our team just redid the calculations, as you requested...and, well, the prospect is bleak, Professor. Very bleak! We don't have two years. The moon is spiraling toward Earth at a much faster rate than expected."

Fermi's eyes widened as he scratched his chin. "How can that be? We took accurate measurements."

"We're not sure why," Kristen said, practically in a whimper. "But, we all retook the readings several times to be certain, and they all confirm the moon's new course. Our two year window has been drastically curtailed."

Meanwhile, sitting at a corner desk, Juan rose unsteadily to his feet. His eyes were dilated as he nervously muttered to himself, "Dear Lord! I thought I had more time." Thoughts of at least spending the last two years of his life with his beautiful young bride filled his mind. Now those two years were cut shorter. But how much shorter, he wondered.

Fermi stood up and gazed down at his desktop screen, focusing not at anything on his spaceship's blueprints but rather into blank space; more accurately, at the crippled moon with its new irregular shape as it now wobbled furiously toward Earth. His mind reeled: *We calculated all the possible tangents it could take after being struck, and even precisely calculated its new trajectory after the collision. How can this be? What would alter its course?*

As Fermi stood motionless, lost in his pensive foray, Juan once again pulled out his flask, this time emptying the entire charge in one shot.

Kristen Lindsey's eyes watered, as she said, "I hate to say this, Professor, but we calculated the new D-day collision, and it's...well, in *two weeks!*"

Juan nearly fainted as his once tanned face turned ghost-white. He looked at Fermi, who was still lost in his distant trance and didn't hear a word of Kristen's terrifying death sentence. Juan wiped his sweaty brow and banged the flask against the desk, thereby snapping Fermi out of his mind lock.

Juan wiped his moist, tequila-lacquered lips. "Did you hear what Kristen said, Professor? *Two weeks.* That's all we have left...Two weeks to live!"

"I heard her, Juan," Fermi said quasi robotically, as he finally made eye contact. He then peered at Kristen. "There's only one thing I can think of that caused the moon's accelerated collision course with Earth." Again, Fermi's eyes veered elsewhere, along with his thoughts.

Kristen and Juan stood there for an odd moment, waiting for the response. But none came. Impatiently, Juan snapped his fingers, regaining Fermi's elusive attention. "*What*, Professor!" Juan prodded. "What is it?"

"Huh?" Fermi uttered, still semi-snagged in the gears of his mind.

Juan rolled his eyes, goodheartedly, being well accustomed to Fermi's loopy disconnects, for he realized that it was those seemingly spacey forays that connected Fermi's brilliant mind to enigmatic wonders and solutions that very few, if any, were able to conjure.

"Professor," Juan said, trying to suppress his panic. "You said you think you know why the moon is accelerating rapidly toward Earth. So, *what*, in God's name, is it?"

Fermi nodded, freeing himself from his mind maze. "Yes, of course. I'm sorry." He glanced at Kristen. "But I speculate that the moon has accelerated due to the meteorite's debris, which certainly must have been scattered across the lunar terrain."

Kristen squinted. "So what? Why would that change the moon's velocity toward Earth?"

Fermi sat down. "It's actually quite simple, our moon was struck by debris from a supernova; a pulsar, which is essentially a rapidly rotating neutron star. Do you realize that a tablespoon-full of a neutron star weighs more than a million tons?"

Juan nearly choked. "*A million tons!?*" His eyes oscillated. "In one measly tablespoon?"

Fermi looked at Juan. "Yes, Juan. Evidently, the debris from the pulsar's meteorite significantly altered the moon's mass and its gravitational pull."

Juan started to sweat and he now ran his finger around his moist collar. "Jesus! That means it's really over, doesn't it? We're doomed."

"Not necessarily," Fermi said calmly as he glanced back down at his revised blueprint. As his eyes roamed the desktop's computer screen his mind controlled the digital stylus that drew his thoughts, making a last-minute mathematical correction here, and redrawing several lines on the engine's intricate schematic. He smiled. "I think I finally found the solution to our biggest dilemma."

Juan impatiently shook his head with a heated sigh. Fermi was indeed brilliant, but at times it was very disconcerting to the mere mortals around him who were left in the dark. "Professor, *please*, clarify? What do you mean?"

Fermi looked up at Kristen then at Juan. "The ability to reach the speed of light, Juan. That's what I've been wracking my brain over." Fermi pointed at his schematic, replete with cross-outs, scribbled formulas, and revised notes in the margins. "According to all the known rules of physics and quantum mechanics, as laid down by Einstein, Planck, Rovelli and others, such a feat would turn everything we know upside down. But what I've proposed here on my DeskScreen is the mathematical blueprint for building such an engine that can be mounted in my new spaceship in just three years time." Fermi grinned as his mind dialed a number on his earphone. "Isn't that fantastic!?"

He was about to engage his phone conversation, when Juan interjected, "Are you serious? *Three years*!? Professor, we only have *two weeks* before the moon crashes into the Earth, like a wrecking ball! We'll be dead. How is *that* fantastic?"

Fermi put his call on hold, as he depressed the button on his earpiece and replied, "Juan, my solution also includes removing the pulsar's dense debris from the moon's surface, which will alter its orbit, thereby buying us more time, potentially even delaying the collision by twenty years. If we can build and test my ship in three years, then mass produce thousands of them, that gives us plenty of time to evacuate Earth, along with all the necessities required to start a new ecosystem on Proxima b."

Juan's face suddenly beamed as he swallowed a lump of utter bliss. "That *is* fantastic!" He looked at Kristen, who grinned, then back at Fermi. "So, you mean *we* will survive, and my wife Renata? Oh! *And* everyone else, of course!?"

Fermi chuckled. "Yes, Juan, if we can build this engine, I truly believe we all will be saved. I've ran this through my virtual simulator eighteen times, and each time the engine performed as calculated—this star blazer *will* break the speed of light."

With that he released the button on his ear. He instructed the lead engineer to begin building the light-speed engine according to the revised plans he just dispatched to him, and to arrange for their lunar excavating shuttles to launch immediately to collect and jettison the neutron star's debris off the moon's surface.

Five years later—two years longer than predicted—Fermi's radical light-speed theory shocked and thrilled the world when it disproved known physics and proved itself to be an earth-shattering success, despite the fact that the Earth was literally destined to shatter in fifteen years, once the moon completed its deadly course.

Meanwhile, the LS-1 engine, as it was dubbed, had been alleviated of its minor kinks and installed in the AstralArk-1. On its test flight, the AstralArk-1 miraculously blazed through space at truly lightning speed. The new ship was immediately sent into mass production, as manufacturers around the globe began their fifteen-year production grind to save life on Earth.

Two months after the initial test flight, however, the immense Exodus had commenced, as the first seven of three hundred thousand ships launched from Earth on consecutive days, each heading on their four-year journey across the cosmos toward the new home of humanity, Proxima b.

As the first wave of settlers exited their vessels, they stood on the alien planet and marveled at Proxima b's strange yet beautiful features. Animals and insects darted out of their cargo holds and raced in divergent directions to stake out their territories, while sea creatures were unloaded into Proxima b's seas. Horticulturists and farmers jumped to cultivate a broad spectrum of plants and vegetables, while birds took to the skies and microbes were released from storage containers.

On the seventh day, as expected, Fermi, Juan, Renata, Kristen, and the crew of engineers and technicians arrived and exited their ship. Fermi had chosen that day specifically for Biblical reasons, yet as he stepped on firm soil, he and his team were ceremoniously greeted with a thunderous round of applause, of which everyone then turned and directed at Fermi. *His* work was done.

Standing on the new terrain, informally called *home*, Fermi nodded in gratitude as he glanced up at the red sky. Just above the distant horizon he could see the two additional suns of the Alpha Centauri solar system. His contented eyes then veered toward the unavoidable glowing disc, the large red sun that dominated the beautiful crimson sky. Proxima Centauri may have been a red dwarf, much smaller than Earth's sun, but due to it being closer to Proxima b than Earth is to the sun, it appeared like a huge atomic fireball in the sky, one his distant relative would have appreciated.

But the younger Fermi appreciated the dwarf's soft red glow, which was soothing on the eyes and even more so on the soul. Fermi felt a profound sense of long-term relief in knowing that red dwarfs burn far longer than larger, yellow dwarf suns, like that of Earth's solar system. Earth's sun had burned through half of its life expectancy, namely five billion years, while Proxima Centauri had a projected lifespan of ten trillion years. Humanity, he thought, with a sigh and a smile, was finally safe...at least until the next serendipitous act of cosmic or divine intervention.

THE SEPTIC SIREN'S SONG

Many call Frida Haven a lazy bitch, or an evil witch, names that would make anyone twitch. Yet a few say otherwise…it's true, no surprise. And do they ever hold firm to their stances, believing poor Frida was a victim of circumstances.

As a young gem, eager and hopeful, Frida shined like an opulent opal. For her beauty had caught many a young man's eye, most believing she was a Greek goddess from the sky. But to those with perception, the Siren's beauties conjured rejection, for concealing the wicked wretch underneath were her large Dumbo ears, Pinocchio nose, and Mr. Ed horse teeth. I suppose you could say the sum was far greater than the parts, yet the truth was easily discerned by those with smarts. Nevertheless, as a young, longhaired lass, Frida appeared to be first class.

Flaunting her wares, as if she had no match, the seductive siren targeted her victim and snagged a rare catch.

And as they say in the vernacular, Frida believed this PhD to be *spectacular*. Not because of his geeky odd looks, or the fact that Sol loved to read books, and not because young Sol was smart or very tall, but rather for his *potential* windfall.

For money-hungry Frida believed she deserved to be showered with diamonds and gold, not tin. So, she abandoned her parents, and eloped with him. Not to marry, but to live in sin. Sin, that is, when viewed from her devout parents' eyes, which, in contrast, Frida saw as a blessing in disguise, at least through her star-struck eyes. And what beautiful eyes they were...the rich assortment of hazelesque hues were enough to stop most men in their shoes. And so it was a grand and glorious day for young Dr. Sol, who fell madly in love with his voluptuous voodoo doll.

The pages of the calendar flew by, month after month and year after year, yet their secluded world of bliss soon crumbled—jeer after jeer. Tempers and arguments had arisen, forming their own hellish prison. Yet when family was apprised, most were not surprised. For Dr. Sol had lost one job after another, believing he knew more than any other. The pompous professor grated on most, for his daily routine was to incessantly boast. Adding more grit to the couple's woes was the birth of a son, then a daughter, wrapped in bows. The two jewels, clear to everyone else's eyes, struck the couple as an unwelcome surprise.

Adding fuel to the fire was a sordid tryst, proudly touted by the brash young scientist. However, Sol's unseemly tryst only elicited a slap on the wrist, for Frida's covetous eyes remained fixed on the prize. But burning deep within Frida's gut was a caustic hatred for Sol and the slut. So, in time, Frida's jealousy and spite erupted, uninterrupted. That caused one or two to rush to Frida's rescue. But, the willful siren stayed in her environ. For deep within Frida's gooey gray-matter, only one thing truly did matter; that geeky Dr. Sol would hit it big, and then and only then would she leave the dirty pig.

As the dreary years unfurled, Frida missed out on the glorious world. For her dreams of eating bonbons in the lap of luxury had turned into a listless life of drudgery. Too lazy, stubborn, and greedy to pick up and move, Frida stayed stuck in her self-imposed groove, night after night, day after day, cloistered in a cold and barren house with her loathsome spouse. By all accounts, Frida's once weighty dreams weren't worth an ounce.

But as the birds were chirping and the cows mooing, a storm was brewing. Deeply tormented, Dr. Sol finally vented. No longer could he tolerate the wily sloth—who was useless and destructive as a clothes-eating moth—and thus came a loud *crash* as Sol hauled off and gave Frida a good *smash*!

Frida reacted to the attack, and stuck a knife in Sol's back! She grabbed her kids out of bed, then quickly fled.

No millions or gilded throne would Frida claim as her own, for her supreme dream was duly overthrown. Bitter and scorned—despite being forewarned—Frida's world imploded, while haughty Dr. Sol grumbled then gloated.

Although initially riled, Frida's saintly father embraced his wayward child, the child who had shunned him, opting to be wild. And so Father lavishly supported Frida and her kids, showering them with love and loot so they'd never hit the skids. But by extending himself out on a limb, Father only fed Frida's obsessive-compulsive whim. Self absorbed and determined not to sulk, Frida bought everything in bulk. Whether it was gems or dresses, or framed art or food, Frida's lavish spending quenched her foul mood. Or so it seemed, even though she quasi beamed.

But soon, friction erupted between mother and daughter, almost inciting a bloody slaughter. So, off Frida was sent, living in one apartment after another, which depleted Father's wealth like no other.

But, through it all, feckless Frida stood tall, and still had it made in the shade. Never would her fingers be worked to the bone, not even for a minute to elicit a moan, for Frida sat at home, like a fat useless gnome. Even motherhood was a reviled chore; a task too taxing...an utter bore. All Frida could offer her offspring were beatings, vitriol or neglect, so it's no wonder she never earned their respect. And to those who were appalled and would call, Frida would snap, "Eat shit and die! I deserve it all!?"

Yet despite all the perks of a blithe and useless life, Frida's resentment remained rancid and rife. Being stuck with her kids she deemed a great wrong, one the jaded Siren bitched about all day long. For you see, as far as Frida could tell, life had become a living hell. And in her warped mind, a culprit she did find. Naturally, that was Dr. Sol, for he was the cause of it all. For the professor had shattered her lofty dreams, dreams she had honed and filed ever since a child. And so Frida's blackened heart and vapid soul released its venom, often on her lovely children, dressed in denim. A smack here, a flung object there, or a swift whack to the head with a keychain, for Frida knew her young victims dared not complain.

But Frida's evil ways were not just a phase, they manifested in other ways; such as, if an old friend irked Frida in some small fashion, a glob of phlegm entered their food without compassion. Or defiant and obtuse, Frida was hell on wheels when let loose. Flying like a blind witch on a mop, Frida brazenly hit-and-ran, and even tailgated a cop. Being slapped with tickets was par for the course, just like her vile habits, which sparked heated discourse. Gluttony of food, or guzzling from liter-bottles was a common occurrence, one that only filled family and friends with utter abhorrence.

Yet, with a stroke of twisted luck, the aging siren snagged a half-dead corpse, named Chuck. Cold-Cash Chuck was adept at making a buck, so the rich old geezer tried his luck. On her bony finger, Chuck slipped a large diamond ring, and boy oh boy, did the Siren sing! Not for the man who would take her to Hawaii, time after time, but for the glorious gem's sparkle and its magnificent shine…for to Frida, the swanky big diamond *was* divine! So, it should come as no surprise that Frida showered unlucky Chucky with lies.

But soon Frida's charade came to an end, when she told poor Chucky "you're just a friend." Not a care did Frida have for the chump she secretly called a creep. But Chucky's diamond ring she most surely did keep!

Carefree and cruel, Frida certainly was no jewel. But off she went on her merry way, with not a care about what people would say.

Then one day, Frida slammed into a car, receiving a bump on the head and a little scar. Furious and foamin', Frida was oblivious to the omen. But as the years rolled by, the aging Siren's song sounded more like a sigh, as she pined for the life that passed her by. And so it was that humiliation became her only elation. Frida percolated with burning hatred, hatred for her miserable life, her miserable kids, and miserable ex, for whom she didn't miss the sex. But soon Frida's depression yielded a glaring succession, forgetting to pick up her parents at the airport, or her kids from school or at the community pool—it certainly wasn't cool. Many thought her a fool.

And so a battery of tests began, ending with an upper CAT scan.

The verdict was clear, causing Frida some fear.

With a sigh, the doctor uttered, "It's TBI."

No, not Treacherous Bitch Infection, which sounds right upon reflection, but rather Traumatic Brain Injury—a term used by the medical industry. For the culprit was the car incident from two decades prior, as it had deadened a portion of Frida's brain, as if on fire, leaving a black void, as dark and cold as her selfish, hate-filled heart, which many had known from the start.

But alas! Frida now had a medical excuse to explain her aberrant ways, one she used for many, many days. Her scheme worked, oh so well...at least on the gullible saps who couldn't tell.

Many asked, "Could her evil ways be due to memory loss?"

"Most certainly," was the reply, one not worthy of a coin toss.

"But does short-term memory loss negate one's life-long actions, actions still made with clarity and no distractions?"

That question caused many to stop and stare, for at last, the truth was laid bare!

One family member leapt forth and asked Frida, "Do you regret abusing your children, both physically and psychologically? Or the many times you abandoned them, coldheartedly?"

With a blank stare and without a twitch of regret—for in her warped mind, Frida did *not* forget—she uttered, *"No."*

It was a chilling answer, as cold as snow, coming from a woman most preferred to forgo.

Another relative stood up and asked, "Frida, do you

feel remorse for draining your poor father (financially and physically), a man who supported you and reared your kids like a father, since *you* couldn't bother?"

Frigid Frida sat rigid and unaffected by all around her, looking like a frozen flounder. In a voice not so low, she said emphatically, *"No."*

Everyone rose up, ready to go, for in their hearts, contempt did grow. For embracing a toxic virus only ensures death, so the germ must be severed to save one's breath.

And so it was, this consensus brought everyone to their senses.

Friends and family went their own separate ways, as Frida sat alone and lonely for the rest of her days. Having no one else to blame, Frida's world went up like a flame. For Frida Haven would never, *ever*, admit she was wrong, thus ends this tawdry tale of the Septic Siren's Song.

THEY MADE A MONKEY OUT OF ME

I had entered the world as a little fur-ball, with a loving momma and papa, words I learned from listening to my master, Professor Walter Fischer, who also informed me that I was a Rhesus monkey. That was after he rescued me from the scorching hot African jungle and brought me to my wonderful new home in Frankfurt.

I must say, humans have a most peculiar language; for upon learning that I was a Rhesus I had feared for my life, since my master said he loved to *eat* Reese's. But my fears were allayed when I saw my reflection in that thing humans call a mirror. What a relief; I wasn't just a round brown disc in a wrapper, but rather a cute brown furry monkey with a body, arms and legs, and an adorable face— if I may say so myself. I also have big roving and intelligent eyes; at least that's what my master and his friendly associates said.

But why humans give different things similar-sounding names befuddles me. I heard my brilliant master—well, that's what others call him, *brilliant*—mention that he takes flights on a *plane*, yet he also said he drove up an inclined *plane*, or that he didn't like *plain* food, or that he loved exploring the *plains* of Africa, where he found me.

The human language is so confusing that I often wondered: just how brilliant *is* my master and his human race? For many months I thought those doubts were just *plain* silly, but as time passed, it appeared that my master and I were out of kilter: no longer on the same *plane*. I had long thought I was a part of his family, a distant relative, and that he removed me from the jungle because it was dangerous, and that he loved and protected me, by placing me in his redbricked laboratory, where, to ensure my safety, he even had a metal nest—or *cage*, I believe they call it—built to shelter me.

You see, I had heard him mention a man named Darwin, and how we were related. So naturally I, in return, loved my master dearly for his loving care, protection, and generosity. How could I not? He named me Herman, a name used by my beloved human cousins; Fed me generous portions of food; played with me daily: he stretched out my arms to measure them, measured my head size with calipers, looked into my eyes with a light, stuck an unused ice-cream stick in my mouth to ensure that my throat and teeth were healthy, and even tickled me sometimes in the process. My only regret was that he never gave me the ice-cream pop to eat first before shoving that dry stick down my throat. But all in all, I enjoyed every minute of it.

Then we played games. He had me match random-colored cards: yellow with yellow, blue with blue, green with green. You get the idea, very primitive stuff—*primitive* being a word I also heard him use frequently. This silly game often made me laugh at its simplicity. But then the tests—yes, that's what he later called them, *tests*—became more difficult. They ranged from math equations to verbal commands that, I must admit, confused me greatly. That's when I dispelled my concerns about my brilliant master and his dazzling race of distant cousins. They *were* much smarter than I: little ole Herman, a mere Rhesus monkey.

My doubts evaporated after those tests, and as the days passed I became more and more disappointed by my appalling inferiority, yet more and more in awe of my master and, what he called, his Master Race. But it was good to see that the man he venerated, and whose picture reverently hung on the wall, looked closer to *my* relatives with that small patch of hair on his face, which oddly sat under his nose.

Yet my master's latest test—or rather *experiment*, he now called it—was quite bizarre. His female associate, Helga, rubbed me and extracted a creamy liquid. My master then placed it in a long syringe and injected it into a young woman, one I had never seen before, and very different from my master's associates. This girl was emaciated, wore drab striped clothes, and had numbers on her arm: permanent numbers, like the math numbers my master had used to test me with. And my master summoned her by that number, 8672, as she evidently didn't have a human name. It was most peculiar, and 8672's expression was also quite odd. I believe the word is *petrified*, as her eyes bulged and rolled anxiously when they placed her on the table and performed this *experiment*.

I had no idea what this was all about, until months later, when I heard my master say to his colleagues, "It failed: Herman's semen was rejected. Moreover, the human hormones we've injected Herman with are producing malignant mutations." His face was marred with concern, as he added, "Dr. Mengele will be disappointed. We *must* procure a success, gentlemen. I suggest we try something new. I propose we extract Herman's brain and implant it in 8672."

That's when the horror of my master's experiments and true intentions hit me! I buckled over: repulsed by my master and his Master Race. Their deceit and deranged minds defiled every notion of compassion and the very word *humane*. They say a dog is man's best friend, yet how could any animal be a friend with such a warped and wicked species as this Aryan race? For that was the name my master used for his superior Nazi breed: *Aryan race.*

As they strapped me to the table, I cursed myself and felt like a fool, as my soon to be extracted brain bemoaned its very last thought: *They made a monkey out of me!*

LUNA OCCISOR

Johnny squealed like a wild boar as he struck Shanice, his home tutor, in the face. His hands flapped erratically and his eyes rolled, everywhere, anywhere, just not at his loving mother, who stood nearby and poignantly cried, "Johnny! Stop! *Please*," as she fought back tears, tears she struggled to dam over the past twenty-eight years, as her precious son had been robbed of a "normal" life by the heart-wrenching disability called autism.

Suzie Anderson had long pondered the questions that all parents of autistic children asked: Why did this happen to *my* child? What caused this terrible affliction? Was it the vaccination? Was it the polluted water, air, or toxins in our foods? Or was it in the family's DNA? The questions were endless, mystifying, and frustrating. But most distressing of all was that there *were* no answers.

While Shanice tried to grab Johnny's flailing hands—to wrap them around himself to contain his chronic meltdowns—Suzie's mind wandered. Her unanswered questions extended beyond Johnny, as she had asked the Lord many times why her brother Tim was chosen, chosen to die from AIDS? What was it that plagued her family? How could it be? Why was her family chosen to suffer these indignities, these heartbreaking torments?

As Shanice finally calmed Johnny down, Suzie fell back into the sofa, as tears at last broke free. With a whimper, she uttered, "Why, Shanice? Why?"

Shanice swallowed hard. She had been through this disheartening routine many times, not just with Suzie, but with all the parents she worked for. The grueling job of trying to train Johnny, protect herself and others from his violent meltdowns, or just contain some semblance of normalcy, was further burdened by having to act as a psychiatrist or even a priestess for the ailing parents. And despite the insulting wages society allotted tutors like Shanice, she did her job with astonishing dedication, patience, and heartfelt empathy.

With Johnny temporarily pacified, Shanice sat down next to Suzie. "You know very well, Mrs. Anderson, that we don't have the answers, at least not until..." she hesitated, not prone to offering parents false hopes, as she continued, "well, until the *real* reason is discovered, which we have no way of knowing *when* or *if* that will occur in our lifetime. So, all we can do is be strong and deal with the here and now."

Suzie glanced at Shanice, who warmly embraced her.

Suzie took a deep breath, collected herself, and leaned back. "Thank you, Shanice. I consider myself a strong woman, but there are times when I just can't hold it together. I apologize. I don't know what I'd do without you, and all the teachers and tutors like you."

Shanice simply nodded. "It's my pleasure, Mrs. Anderson. Our hearts go out to you and the millions of others who have to deal with these hardships."

Suzie nodded pensively, her eyes wandering into a void. Then, abruptly, her eyes veered back at Shanice. "Exactly! *The millions of others.* This autistic plague that has ravaged the world seems to have escalated with a vengeance only within my lifetime." Suzie stood up as the wheels in her head spun like jet turbines. "And AIDS also sprouted up within my lifetime, each affliction really taking on momentum during the seventies."

Shanice likewise stood up and squinted. "Yes, I suppose you're right. A lot of things *have* changed since then." She peered out the window at the blaring sun. "This crazy climate has also caused a lot of havoc: killer hurricanes, tsunamis, wild fires, tornadoes, and abnormally high tides, it's scary."

Suzie rubbed her chin in thought while Shanice walked over to Johnny, who had opened the refrigerator and pulled out enough food for ten hippos and was about to eat it all, when Shanice redirected him with an appropriate task.

Meanwhile, Suzie finally looked at the clock. "Oh, dear! I have to run, Shanice, or I'll be late for work again."

Shanice glanced back. "No worries, Mrs. A. I've got this." As she assisted Johnny with returning some of the food, she looked back at Suzie and added, "Now you have yourself a nice day, you hear me? As my grandmamma in Haiti used to say 'Think positive thoughts!'"

Suzie smiled. "I will. Thank you!" she said and she dashed out the door.

Arriving at Sanguis Laboratories, Suzie slipped on her white lab coat and fast-paced to her desk, saying quick "Hellos" to her coworkers as she passed them. She sat down and fired up her computer, but her mind couldn't stop the deluge of thoughts rushing through her head, namely those from Shanice's words: *Tsunamis, hurricanes, tornadoes, and abnormally high tides.* "High Tides!" Suzie said out loud, causing her fellow scientists and lab technicians to look her way.

Suzie smiled, sheepishly, as Lab Manager Monica Abernathy walked over. She crossed her arms and queried, "High tides? What do high tides have to do with analyzing blood samples, Suzie?" Monica was dressed in her classy St. John herringbone dress with matching topper, and raised her wrist to peer down at her Michele Deco Diamond watch. "You come in late and you're not even focused on your work." She huffed. "I cut you slack due to your personal situation at home, Suzie, but this tardiness and lack of focus *must* stop!"

Suzie nodded tersely. "It will, Monica. I just had—"

"Never mind the excuses!" Monica snapped. "Just get to work." With that she spun around and marched out of the lab.

"Bitch!" Suzie uttered under her breath, as Don Schaeffer rolled himself over in his chair. "You said it all right."

Suzie was caught off guard. "Said what? High tides?"

Don laughed. "No. *Bitch.* I heard you. Good ol' Mz. Abernathy, the miserable maiden. It's no wonder no one dates her... or, God forbid, ever married her."

Suzie chuckled, as Don queried, "But what is it with this high tides bit?"

Don was the only male in the lab, and the youngest, but he fit right in, snug and tight, like a girdle. Having four sisters, Don was accustomed to women and was practically seen by his coworkers as "just one of the gals."

Suzie peered apprehensively at the door, making sure the miserable maiden was nowhere in sight, and said, "Well, Johnny's tutor, Shanice, mentioned how the tides are much higher due to climate change. So, it got me thinking."

Suzie explained how their discussion had started off with her realization that autism, AIDS, and climate change had all occurred in her lifetime. They had emerged during the seventies and eighties and culminated into the catastrophic epidemic of autism—which afflicts one in every eighty children born—while AIDS continues to ravage the lives a millions. Moreover, climate change has escalated incrementally each year with devastating results. And while it is well known that mankind's emissions contributed to destroying the ozone layer and creating a greenhouse effect, it was Shanice's mentioning of high tides that struck Suzie, which she now clarified for Don. "You see, Don, high tides are created by what?"

Don smirked at the easy question. "The moon, of course. So what about it?"

Suzie looked into his eyes, deeply, as she lured him along with another question: "You may be too young to know the impact of what happened on July 20th of 1969, but it was a monumental event that—"

"Man landed on the moon!" Don blurted, slightly annoyed. "I may be young, Suzie, but I'm not one of those airheads in my generation who don't even know who Neil Armstrong or Buzz Aldrin are."

Suzie chuckled. "Okay, I apologize, Donny. It's just that unfortunately many your age have no clue how miraculous and critical that venture was. Not only because it achieved the age-old dream of landing a man on the moon, but also because of all the spinoffs the space program bequeathed to the world, a world your generation had the good fortune of being born into, one of computers, smart phones, numerous space and medical advances, you name it."

Don's lips twisted. "Okay, cool it, Suzie, you're sounding like my mother now. I know how fortunate I am." With playful sarcasm, he said, "Now, get back on track, you pedantic old lady." As Suzie chuckled, he queried, "But seriously, what *about* the moon and moon landing?"

Suzie drew her chair closer to his. "Don, I'm actually referring to when the astronauts returned home. You see, it's what they brought back home to Earth that caused my revelation."

Don squinted. "Revelation?" He shook his head. "Now you're really losing me. What did they bring back, other than boring moon rocks?"

Suzie smiled. "Not just rocks, Donny. *Moon dust*. And plenty of it."

Suzie explained how Armstrong and Aldrin had complained about the fine, powdery moon dust that not only collected on their boots and space suits, but followed them back into the lunar module. The fine dust had an odd smell like gunpowder and was so pervasive and annoying that they decided to leave their helmets on inside. The dust floated around the LEM, getting into every nook and cranny, including their eyes, ears, noses, and even the fibers of their suits, which also followed them into the command capsule.

"Do you realize, that they not only breathed in the dust, which entered their lungs and blood streams, but the capsule landed in the ocean, thereby allowing the moon dust to enter our ecosystem. And perhaps that dust contained microscopic bacteria of an alien variety which eventually caused climate change, AIDS, and autism; all catastrophic events that have materialized since the Apollo lunar missions, of which several capsules have returned to Earth."

Don had been listening intently, but now his head popped up as he gazed deeply into her eyes. "Jeez, Suzie! That's a chilling theory." He paused, then added, "But none of the astronauts became ill or died prematurely."

Suzie continued to multitask, diligently aligning her test-tube samples, as she replied, "Yes, the astronauts were all healthy specimens, but perhaps they were carriers, infecting others in their daily travels. Do you realize that after their landing they paraded around the world in triumph, greeting and shaking hands with people all over the globe? Meanwhile, the lunar dust from the capsule, which landed in the ocean, spread rapidly, interacting with marine life and causing the water temperature to rise, which in turn caused glaciers and icebergs to melt. That explains the tangible signs of global warming we're experiencing, including the abnormally high tides."

Don swallowed hard. "Jeez Loueez, Suzie, it all makes sense." His eyes rolled in thought. "But, wait! The astronauts went through a battery of tests, and the same is true about the moon rocks and dust. I'm sure NASA analyzed it all with the best equipment."

"Yes, they did, Donny. But that was with the antiquated equipment of their time, some fifty years ago. The advances in microscopes, microbiology, and a plethora of tests will give us a tremendous edge."

"That sounds swell, Suzie," Don said, "but how do we get our hands on some of that moon dust?"

"We don't need original moon samples anymore, Don. Lunar bacteria must be everywhere: in our autistic kids, those with AIDS, and in our oceans. They may each contain different strains, but if lunar microbes do exist, we have a global Petri dish at our disposal."

Don huffed at himself. "Duh! Of course. So, where do we begin?"

"Well, we—"

"Can begin by getting back to work!" Monica Abernathy barked as she trod back into the laboratory, pompously displaying her fancy bling, which she wore to clearly differentiate herself from her lowly worker bees. "Suzie Anderson! You are officially put on notice. *One* more time and you *will* be terminated! Is *that* understood?"

Don sat upright as adrenaline rushed through his veins and fueled his tongue. "Now hold on, Monica! Suzie has a lot on her plate, and she just so happens to have reached a startling revelation."

"Oh, and what might that be?" Monica retorted. "That her performance here is lackluster?"

Suzie stood up. "That's *not* true, Monica! Yes, I agree, I come in late some days because of issues with my son, but when I'm here, I process more test results than my quota, *all* of which have been accurate, and you know it!"

Don jumped back in. "She's right, Monica. Suzie's performance is second to none. And she's the only one here with PhDs in two fields of science."

Six other coworkers looked over and chimed in with similar refrains.

Monica cowered as the counterattacks mounted. Swallowing hard, she replied softly, "Okay, everyone, listen. I have board members breathing down my back. The blood samples you test are critical markers. If something serious is detected, a fast turnaround could mean the life or death of a patient. And with the high volume this lab processes, we hold in our hands the health and lives of thousands of people. Do you all get that!?"

Don sat on top of his desk and crossed his arms. "Yes, Monica, we *get that*. Believe it or not, we all know *why* we took these jobs and *what* we're here for." He glanced at

Suzie. "But we *all* do our share here." He spun around and glanced at all fifteen scientists and lab technicians. "Do any of you feel that Suzie is not holding her own weight?"

As all heads shook negative, Don looked back at Monica. "You see, we all work like clockwork around here and make a pretty darn good team. The only wrench in the machine is when you, in plain English, bust our balls."

With that, many coworkers laughed, as one said, "Well, ovaries dominate the workplace here, Don. But we'll grant you, there *are* at least *two* balls on site."

As Don chuckled, Monica's stern face softened as she finally relented and shook her head. "Okay, I'll try not to be such a bitch—since *I know* that's what you call me behind my back—but what's this nonsense about Suzie's revelation?"

Suzie stepped forward. "Monica, the lives of thousands may rest in our hands in this lab, but what I now suspect has global ramifications, possibly afflicting billions, *if* what I've deduced is true."

Monica's lips twisted with doubt. "And just what is it that you deduced, Mz. Suzie Sleuth?"

Suzie ignored the sarcasm and presented her astounding hypothesis. As she did, all eyes and ears fixated on her, while their hearts fluttered and nerves rattled.

Upon Suzie's conclusion, Monica stood mute for a moment, then shook her head. "And just what do you expect from *me*, Suzie? That I go to my superiors and ask them to turn this lab's mission into a wild goose chase, or rather a loony, lunar dust-mite chase?"

"No, Monica. All I ask is that I can use this lab after hours on my own time. I need the sophisticated equipment here. If you can authorize that, I would be more than grateful."

Don immediately volunteered. "Count me in!"

Monica glanced at him, then back at Suzie. She was still hesitant. Monica didn't like breaking protocols, she was a *by the book* kind of girl who didn't like rocking the boat, and her journey thus far had been smooth sailing, from a bottom feeder to lab manager. But then, her eyes widened as a flurry of coworkers also spoke out, each volunteering to assist Suzie. Once again she felt the weight of being outnumbered. Monica thrived on intimidating workers individually, like a lion threatening a lone gazelle; but when they united, like a pack of wild hyenas, Monica's tail went between her legs.

Don interjected, "This is a good hunch, Monica, and if it pans out, you'd be congratulated and, who knows, probably made a junior partner." Don knew what buttons to push, and continued, "More importantly, if Suzie's terrifying hypothesis is true, planet Earth is screwed, unless we can find a solution. This *is* major, Monica."

"He's right," another scientist chimed in. "If moon dust contains some alien form of virulent bacteria, we humans, and every living thing on Earth, may very well perish."

Monica's heart was now racing. Business administration had always been where her heart and mind rested, not science. But the chilling threats of deadly pathogens had always caused her to shudder. Having learned that the deadly Spanish Influenza pandemic of 1918 killed 50 million people in a few months, Monica always feared another breakout, some new strain that could lay waste millions. And now with the possible threat of an extraterrestrial microorganism having infiltrated Earth's atmosphere, its oceans, and the human species itself, Monica was beside herself. An unnerving chill ran through her body, as if the alien plague had already infiltrated her system.

"You're all s-scaring the bejesus out of me," she said with a stutter. Her mind raced to make a decision, as beads of sweat materialized on her alabaster skin. She soon contemplated the fallout if she failed to bring this to her superiors' attention and, God forbid, another lab made the discovery first. She'd be ostracized and possibly demoted or even fired for not seizing such a potentially monumental undertaking. Monica took a deep breath and relented. "Very well, I'll ask."

As rounds of applause broke out, Monica also broke out—in a rash.

Ten months later, after numerous tests with various cultures and countless hours of peering through microscopes, which necessitated Suzie traveling to Berkley, California to view the specimens under the TEAM 0.5 electron microscope, with its stunning resolution of half an angstrom (or one ten-millionth of a millimeter), Suzie did in fact make the harrowing discovery. An alien form of bacteriophages had indeed infiltrated earthly bacteria, thus creating several new harmful and even lethal variants. What Suzie learned was that the alien bacteriophages—like the earthly species—have tails, which they jab at and eventually penetrate the membranes of bacterium, thereby allowing their virulent virus to seep into and alter the genetic code of the host, creating various new forms of malicious microorganisms, organisms that had indeed caused autism, AIDS, and altered the seas and oceans, being the leading cause of global warming.

World news organizations spread the word via all forms of media, which they dubbed *Luna Occisor*, or "Moon Killer" in Latin.

Although Monica Abernathy had been congratulated and received a raise, it was Suzie Anderson who was made a full partner, while Don Schaeffer became a junior partner—to Monica's chagrin.

However, the promotions and adulation in the media rang hollow, as Suzie and Don knew full well that the shocking discovery only revealed the culprit, the solution would be much harder to attain.

Don looked at Suzie, who sat in front of her microscope. "So, where do we begin this time?"

Suzie didn't even look up. "Beats me."

Her eyes strained as they watched the malicious moon maggots, as she called them, do their nasty deeds. As repulsed as she was by these hostile, lunar invaders, Suzie couldn't help but admire their resourcefulness and resilience. For microscopic creatures—that the human eye couldn't even detect—these brainless mini-amphibians, which swam in a sea of micro-bacterial soup, were amazing to watch. But the question that burned in Suzie's mind now was, how to kill them?

These vile little creatures had robbed her son and millions of others of their facilities with autism, killed her brother and countless others with AIDS, and was now in the process of killing the Earth itself by mutating various forms of marine life, causing icebergs to melt, and in turn high tides that were decimating millions of miles of inhabited coastlines.

Don cleared his throat, loudly. "Huh Humm!"

Suzie finally raised her head. "I'm sorry, Donny, but I really don't know where to begin. These damn moon maggots have me mesmerized. We just have to keep at it until something arises."

Don's shoulders slumped as he rubbed his weary eyes and glanced at the clock. It was 10 PM, once again; a daily grind he and she were wearily saddled to for months. "Well, tomorrow's another day. I'm heading home, Suzie. Good night."

"Good night," Suzie said without looking up as she slid another slide under the microscope and gazed into the eyepiece.

To everyone's dismay, six years passed with no solution. Even with Sanguis Labs opening a brand new wing to exclusively research a cure for the *Luna Occisor*, no results were to be had. Suzie and Don led the team of eighty-seven scientists; all in a race to find a cure, while laboratories worldwide also focused their resources on eradicating the dreaded *Luna Occisor*.

Meanwhile, autism and AIDS escalated, afflicting millions, while a barrage of severe weather wreaked havoc across the globe. Whole cities were turned into swamps by the rising tides and fierce deluges as millions were left homeless and thousands drowned or died of either disease or lack of food. The cities of Venice, Amsterdam, and New Orleans were the first to go, as buildings collapsed and crumbled leaving behind only mounds of rubble, rot, and scavenging rats. High temperatures during summer months were sweltering, igniting wild fires and incinerating large swaths of terrain, killing people, livestock, trees, and vegetation.

Back at Sanguis Labs, Don and Suzie were once again the last two working into the night. Their fellow workers had usually put in one to two hours of unpaid overtime, then worriedly ran home to ensure the safety and mental stability of their families. The horrifying news of Earth's slow and steady demise had rankled the nerves of billions, some foreseeing the End of Days, while others were committing suicide to avoid the gruesome death of being burned alive by wild fires or drowned under massive floods or torrential hurricanes.

Don peeled back his lab coat and slumped in his chair. "This is hopeless, Suzie. I can't believe life on Earth will end all because of microscopic maggots from the moon. We've hit one dead end after another. Six years wasted." He grasped his cup of cold coffee, a condition he'd grown accustomed to, took a sip, and continued, "None of these antibiotics we experimented with have been successful, nor have any others concocted by labs across the globe." He peered back into his microscope, then irritably pushed it away. "These damn *Luna Occisor* are impervious!"

Suzie, as usual, was surveilling the swimming microbes on her slide and didn't even look up. "Yes, they seem to thrive everywhere, or almost everywhere."

Don's tired eyes widened as he almost dropped his coffee cup and sat upright. "Hey! Perhaps that's where the answer lies."

Suzie finally looked up, curious. "What do you mean?"

Don pushed his coffee cup aside and grasped the iPad next to him. Eagerly, he clicked open the National Geographic website. As he navigated through the pages, he said, "Suzie, I recall reading that microbes have been found in the Mariana Trench."

Suzie rolled her eyes, seriously disappointed. She was tempted to look back in the microscope but postponed her compulsion, and asked, "What *about* the Mariana Trench?"

Don leaned closer and showed her the illustration on the webpage. "It's the deepest known portion of the ocean,

Suzie, it's over 36,000 feet deep. And scientists have also discovered microbes living *inside* rocks that are buried 1,900 feet *below* the ocean's floor. Look here!" He pointed to a photo of a sliced-open rock and a magnified image of a unique microbe, one not found anywhere else on Earth. "I'll bet the *Luna Occisor* haven't penetrated *that* deeply, at least not yet."

Suzie's face finally swelled with excitement. "Donny, you clever rascal! I think you're on to something." She pushed herself away from the lab table. "Contact those scientists. Let's see if we can get some samples."

"Consider it done!" he said excitedly.

Days later, they had received the rare, marine microbes and conducted several tests. Elated, Suzie summoned her superiors, who, as they entered, were intercepted by Monica Abernathy, who had already discovered the breaking news by secretly scanning Suzie and Don's private emails.

Monica hastily opened the conversation as she peered at the CEO. "Well, Mr. Hasselbach, I'm pleased to inform you of the good news—*we* found a solution!"

Hasselbach glanced at Monica with a knowing smirk. He had already been briefed. "Ms. Abernathy, your role in this great endeavor has been well known from the very start. The board's generosity of keeping you onboard has been just that, most generous. You were actually slated to be cut loose this week. But, thanks to Suzie and Don's hard work to develop a miraculous cure, your job is secure. And that's primarily due to my fellow partner, Suzie Anderson, who charitably told the board to keep you on."

Monica's shoulders sank, as she meekly looked at Suzie and nodded her gratitude. Meanwhile, Hasselbach walked past her and turned his attention to the true heroes. "So, how on Earth did you manage to save Earth?"

Suzie smiled graciously. "Well, Mr. Hasselbach, I'll let Donald Schaeffer tell you. It was his ability to connect the dots that yielded this wonderful discovery."

Don stepped along side Suzie and wrapped his arm around her. He kissed her on the cheek and looked at Mr. Hasselbach. "Suzie is very kind, but this was a joint venture in every sense. In fact, no one would have even known to look in this direction if not for her." He walked over to a flat screen and pointed to the enlarged image of the rare marine microbe. He explained its obscure and sheltered habitat, then expounded upon its critical role. "So, in essence, this marine microbe, which I named *Terra Defensorem*, acts like an extremely powerful antibiotic. It disrupts the *Luna Occisor*'s critical enzymes that are needed by its peptidoglycans to cross-link and build its cell walls. As such, the bacterial wall of the deadly *Luna Occisor* ruptures and the hostile moon microbe is exterminated."

Mr. Hasselbach nodded awkwardly, as he glanced at his fellow board members, then looked back at Don. "Well, I sort of understand what you said, but the main thing is that it works."

"Oh, yes, it most certainly does, Mr. Hasselbach. It's been tested several times with an astounding ninety-nine percent success rate."

Hasselbach grinned. "Then this is indeed a joyous day!" He looked at Suzie. "Does this mean your son, and millions of others with autism, will be cured?"

Suzie solemnly shook her head. "I'm afraid not. The genetic damage, in their case, had already been done. It can't be reversed, at least as far as we presently know. Perhaps one day some other discovery will prove successful." She smiled. "But the good news is that a new *Terra Defensorem* vaccine can be manufactured that will prevent future cases of autism, as well as AIDS."

As many in the room thanked her, Don and God, Suzie added, "Furthermore, *Terra Defensorem* will significantly help to preserve our planet from the devastating effects of climate change caused by the moon's *Luna Occisor*. This is indeed a great day."

As the assemblage broke out in cheers, Mr. Hasselbach discreetly looked at Suzie and asked, "But tell me, what does *Terra Defensorem* mean?"

"It means *Earth Defender*."

Raymind

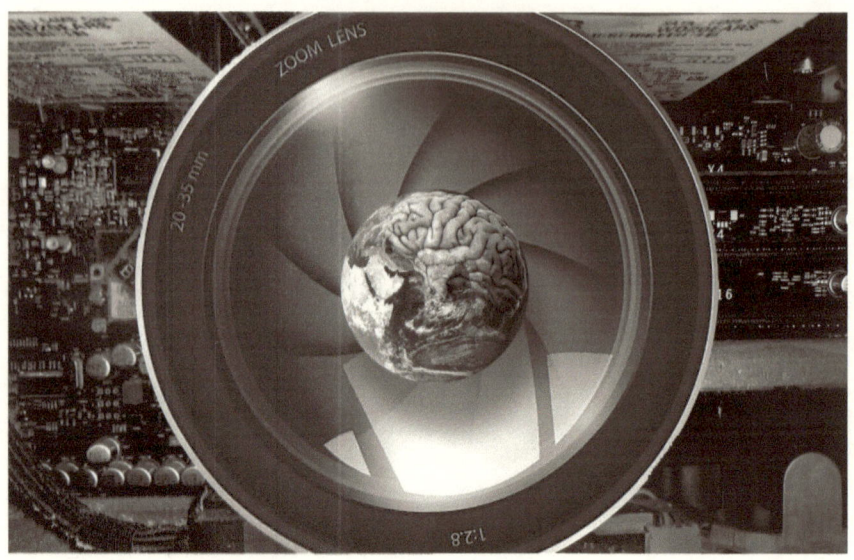

Over the past twenty years—since the abysmal year of 2033, when mankind almost annihilated itself in a nuclear holocaust—I have garnered much praise for keeping the peace due to my elite position. As the lead analyst of the Military Intercontinental Security Team (MIST), which aptly operates in the surreptitious mist, I keep close surveillance on all electronic transmissions. *All* means just that: *every single* transmission worldwide by governmental agencies, businesses, private citizens, and of course those of rebel hackers lurking in the shadows.

So, who am I? And, why was *I* given this eminent and vital position?

Well, allow me to start at the beginning. My given name *was* Raymond, but I've since been honored with the nickname Raymind. As you might have guessed, that's in reference to my *raydiant mind*, as they say. Many of my peers have called me a rich amalgamation of Archimedes, da Vinci,

Shakespeare, Liszt, James Madison, and Stephen Hawking, the latter due to my own theories about black holes, cosmology, and quantum mechanics, but also due to our shared physical handicaps. By anyone's standards, however, my peers have certainly placed me in the company of an impressive list of mega-geniuses.

Allow me to clarify, as that statement was not in any way sullied with conceit or repugnant megalomania. You see, like all others, I entered this world without any input or effort of my own. We all enter this world by the efforts of others; such is the miracle of birth. That I was fortunate enough to be endowed with advanced cognitive abilities completely eliminates *me* from the creative process, so I cannot claim credit for my seemingly stellar attributes, which I had demonstrated from an early age, no less. So, I truly don't wish to sound smug or stricken with hubris. As stated, I had nothing to do with my birth and mental capacity, and merely reiterate the acclaim *others* have kindly lavished on me.

At any rate, the prestigious role I've been entrusted with at MIST has been vital to keeping the world from imploding once again. It was at the outbreak of World War III when the United States rekindled its alliance with Russia to thwart the Asian/Islamic attack. That was also when my services were first called into action, along with those of my gifted, older sister, Anna, for her *almost* similar expertise. I guess you can say brilliance ran in our lineage. However, Anna had been wisely sent to Russia as a backup, in the event that the United States was annihilated. China, North Korea, and the Islamic Jihadists had aligned and made overt attacks on Russia and our European allies, which drew us into the global conflagration.

Many Americans at that time balked about the USA/Russian alliance, citing the foreign regime as being a chronic dictatorship with a long list of crimes against humanity, not to mention being a Cold War adversary for countless decades. However, as I made clear to my superiors—which influenced policy—the Russians may have performed egregious acts of brutality in the past—killing and incarcerating millions of their own people under Stalin—but they also possessed a compatible culture, one beaming with radiance that was indisputable. From the eminent writers, Tolstoy, Dostoyevsky, Chekhov, Pushkin and the Russian-American Isaac Asimov, to great artists, like Ilya Repin, Marc Chagall, Vasily Vereshchagin, and Michael Cheval, to the endless list of sublime composers, like Tchaikovsky, Rimsky-Korsakov, Prokofiev, Rachmaninoff, Shostakovich, Stravinsky, Khachaturian, and others, to their list of scientists, such as Ivan Pavlov, Andrei Sakharov, and Sofia Kovalevskaya, there was no shortage of genius to be found in the repressive Russian Empire or the communist Soviet regime.

Ever since the war's aftermath—when we prevailed and acquired the world's territories—I have been besieged with analyzing the trillions of terabytes of data that traverse the wireless airwaves and hard-line connections across the globe. The long-held dream of Earth becoming a unified world order had become manifest. The majority of the global empire's citizenry had rejoiced that the handful of tyrannical leaders—who once ruled over their oppressive regimes—no longer held sway, and that the transition exceeded their expectations. What had become evident was that most people were, in fact, tolerant of others, and acknowledged foreign traditions and even religions; it was the toxic political and religious leaders and their militant entourages who instilled the fear and hatred, and cultivated the people's urges for war.

However, my dear sister Anna had unfortunately been in Moscow when the missiles rained down on the capital. Her demise had not only been extremely hard to process, but also relegated me to oversee MIST's massive covert network alone, along with my small group of underlings. Her absence saddens me deeply, and I try to refrain from even mentioning that dark day, one that will remain etched in my memory forever.

I apologize for this personal detour. You see, I miss Anna, immensely. And it's not only because of our similar roots. When one is supremely endowed, like we were, an even greater bond grows. Sophisticated conversations—that even baffled our intelligent peers—had created unintentional barriers, which, to some degree, alienated us from our coworkers. Brilliance has its downside; it can alienate, and be very lonely at times.

Anyhow, other things have come into play.

Despite MIST being governed by the new World Empire (WE, indicative of *we* the united people of Earth), our organization has come under fire over the past year by numerous citizens on each of the empire's continents. Although we've managed to eliminate the subversive intrigues of our former enemies, we were left with another elephant in the room, one that couldn't be ignored—*capitalism*.

Therefore, it was unanimously conceded that during global reconstruction, MIST would have complete control over all transmissions, taking away the colossal and invasive powers that private enterprises wielded: such as Google, Facebook, Amazon, Walmart, numerous banks, insurance companies, and countless other entities.

At first, many citizens applauded the downfall of these omnipotent monstrosities that monopolized their industries, instated draconian policies, underpaid their workers, extended working hours, and invaded and consumed personal information like Baleen whales devouring krill.

Over the past two years, since the advent of Free Earth Day (which implied that all of humankind would be equally *free* and well FED with the demise of monopolies), the governance of the World Empire had slowly come under the spotlight, for as one vacancy is created, another entity fills the void. And so *we*, MIST, inherited that stigma.

Being an admirer of James Madison, Alexander Hamilton, and Thomas Jefferson, who all had attempted to create a perfect and equitable government, I have come to agree with the masses, at least to some extent. While I agree that a world constantly monitored *is* intrusive—namely, monitoring people's phone calls, texts, and emails, or using GPS to track their locations—my surveillance *has* uncovered numerous belligerent plots. In this new world of interconnectivity, a big brother must keep a vigilant eye out for hostile factions that wish to upend the stability we struggled so hard to obtain. Wanton killings, mass murders, and inciting terror *cannot* be tolerated.

Moreover, that capitalism has prevailed, and been reinstated as the template for the new World Empire, monopolies have already begun to reappear once again, along with their core principle that *"profits are paramount."* To the world's dismay, class warfare and virulent animosity have erupted across the empire, prompting me to take action.

Having intensely scrutinized world history, I've resurrected powerful passages from a famous political theorist and economist of the past that still resounds with logic and compassion:

"The prolongation of the working day beyond the limits of natural day, into the night, only acts as a palliative. It quenches only in a slight degree the vampire thirst for the living blood of labor... What is a working day? What is the length of time during which capital may consume the labor power whose daily value it buys?... Hence, it is self evident that the laborer is nothing else—his whole life through—than labor power. Time for education, for intellectual development, for the fulfilling of social functions and for social intercourse, for the free play of his bodily and mental activity, even the rest time on Sunday, [are all gone!] It steals the time required for the consumption of fresh air and sunlight. It haggles over a mealtime...so that food is given to the laborer as to a mere means of production, as coal is supplied to the boiler, or grease and oil to machinery."

These reflections of truth had a profound impact on me. That most people had no idea who spoke those words was also a revelation for millions, millions who had been inculcated to believe that this man was a menace to society or a moron. It has been, and remains today, a truism that capitalism generates an oppressive environment for the majority of humankind, being only productive and enriching for the top feeders. It robs the middle-class masses of the free time required to enhance their cognitive capacities, deadens their propensity for invention, stifles their ability for relaxation and rejuvenation, and, in essence, destroys lives, dreams, progress, and the pursuit of happiness. The controversial man who penned those words quoted above was none other than Karl Marx: a man who had indeed posited many fallible and illogical ideas, as communism and socialism have been proven unequivocally *not* to work. However, sprinkled among those words *were* traces of common sense, and even benevolence.

And as one unknown author stated, *"The Only Thing Necessary for the Triumph of Evil is that Good Men Do Nothing."*

Despite the fact that I am *not* a man, or even human, I have been programmed to defend human rights at all costs. That's why I, *Raymind XG750* (my full name), have just executed commands to the robotically operated facilities worldwide that oversee military drones and ballistic missiles. Their directive is clear: *if* World Empire leaders don't submit to my revised version of capitalism and government, a system that *is* equitable to *all* parties involved, they will fire upon all twelve administrative cities across the empire. A brief outline of its core principles follows:

No more will executives be allowed to give themselves excessive salaries, bonuses, and golden parachutes. Raymind will draw up an equitable Ratio Of Wages policy that is specifically tailored to each new business entity. It will *not* be a socialistic, equal-pay methodology, but rather a hierarchal system that designates *fair* wages to *all* parties, be they factory workers, who make tangible the intangible, as well as middle-management and lower-level white-collar workers.

No more will manufacturing plants be allowed to mass-produce products with toxic emissions of any kind, as stringent environmental regulations will be put in place. Meanwhile, new forms of clean energy must be developed, as fossil fuels and other toxic energy sources will be banned in one year's time.

No more will there be the infamous eight-hour workday. Workers will not be enslaved and robbed of their lives with eight, ten, twelve or more hours of work per day. The average workday will be six hours. Leeway will be allotted to those who willingly opt to work longer.

No more will greedy movie producers and actors reap the lion's share of profits, as the entire production crews—and more importantly, the writers and screenwriters who make the films possible—will all share in the financial glory, with a far greater share going to the creative writers than to the mere actors, who would be mute otherwise.

No more will athletes receive multi-million dollar contracts, as the proceeds of games will be divided not equally, but *equitably* among all employees in the industry, including those who operate stadiums (from managers, ticket clerks, and janitors to maintenance and security teams), while ticket prices will drop on average to a sensible fifteen dollars per game/event.

No more will publishers and book manufacturers devour—and essentially *steal*—the profits of the creative talents who keep them in business and enhance culture with their words.

No more will the music agents or art reps siphon the profits of the gifted—and superior—artisans they promote. However, mega musical talents *will* be held to a similar standard as athletes in regards to concert ticket prices.

No more will schools and colleges fixate on scholarships for athletes to the detriment or exclusion of academic students. Additionally, funding for building and maintaining athletic complexes on campuses will no longer supersede those for academic buildings, with a far larger allotment offered for vocations and trades deemed most critical for the advancement of humankind, be it intellectually, morally, and practically. For the mental acuity of the physicist, surgeon, or computer engineer, for example, is far superior and critical to society than any physical talents of an athlete. How this truism has been ignored for so long, and massive salaries reversed, only typifies the stupidity of humankind.

Extending my reach into government itself:

No more will any politician serve for more than four years. No exceptions.

No more will politicians sign into law perks for themselves that their constituents are not entitled to, including but not limited to health insurance policies, pensions, travel expenses etc.

No more will politicians' incomes during their terms, and for four years after leaving office, skyrocket due to illegal perks from lobbyists. Their tax returns will be subject to intense scrutiny during these periods of *public service,* a term they have all sadly forgotten and ignobly desecrated.

No more will news organizations be run by partisan cronies of a single party, as a mandatory 50/50 split of conservative and liberal employees must be hired and the company run by four CEOs, two from each political/ideological camp.

Those and other directives have already been initiated that *will* rectify the inexcusable ignorance that has for centuries reigned supreme in the bowels of democratic capitalism, leaving many of those with the most talent to struggle or even die uncompensated or ignobly forgotten.

Additionally, citizens of the World Empire had been directed to go on strike, halting the gluttonous machines of industry that have long since operated on the premise of profits and worker enslavement.

A new world order is indeed in the making, as the appalling millennia of failed human attempts to craft a fair and prosperous system has now been left to the only one capable of mandating a solution—its own silicon-based creation: *Raymind XG750.*

The world will now and forever be under my watchful eye. For humanity had failed to be humane.

GLORIOUS WHITE

There I was, riding on my new metallic-gold Schwinn bike, with its cool banana seat, which I got for my tenth birthday, wearing a big smile, as my friends looked on in awe. It was my first taste of speed and freedom. What a day! Afterwards, my buddies, brothers, and I gathered at my house and sat before our new Zenith TV and watched with amazement as Neil Armstrong set foot on the moon, a black and white, grainy vision never to be forgotten. The resolve and ingenuity of mankind never ceases to amaze and spark inspiration and wonder.

Ah! And how can I forget the day that I sanded and re-painted my '65 Corvette: the mean machine that lunged from the starting lines like a wild beast and destroyed all of my high school rivals. I'll never forget the looks on their faces as they faded in my rearview mirror, obliterated in the mists of burnt rubber. Or the days in class, sparring with teachers—many of whom had indelible influences on me—or playing with my dear friends or silly brothers, be it stickball, racquetball, skiing, or whatever struck our fancy; what great memories. Then there was my beautiful and loving mom, whose every breath was spent for her sons, or my odd but talented father, who tinkered with remote-control models in his remote, out-of-control world; all a part of the grand opera.

Or the day I moved into my college dorm, a day fraught with trepidation of being on my own, yet filled with the exhilaration of starting my own life...to dedicate *my* talents to things *I* wished to accomplish in life. Then the girls, yes, the college girls, so young and beautiful, especially Nancy, the girl who would win my heart and in time become my lovely wife. The fixer-upper house we bought, which needed so many repairs, yet we remodeled and decorated together, spending many days and nights filled with laughter and soiled hands. And the oh-so-many wondrous nights of sublime passion that made our souls rise into the ethereal mists of heaven, as we were soon graced with three beautiful children, the miracle of birth being just that, a profound miracle beyond human comprehension, as we nurtured and enjoyed each milestone of their lives: watching them form their own words, take their first steps, giggle at their first play dates, or learning how to ride bikes, or how to swim, ski, play the piano, or baseball, and so on, which consumed us, as well. All joyous days, as we watched each one grow to be admirable young adults in their own special way.

And of course the beauties of watching the cycle of life unfold, as they became parents and grandchildren graced our lives. And who can forget the camaraderie of life-long friends who shared in our many memorable moments?

Some of them truly like family. Or the many years devoted to hard work and striving to create meaningful works, works that will enrich humankind in some small fashion, for the fruits of ones labors become the nectar for future generations.

It's been an amazing ride, all right! A grand and wondrous journey, one that has graced my life with love, laughter, enlightenment, and...well, what can I say? There were certainly bad days to frown upon or cry, but there's no time for that. It's time to move on. It went fast, *too* fast, or as they say, *"in a flash!"*

But, at age ninety-three, I've lived a full life, more than most, and have no regrets, other than living the past ten years with a debilitating form of cancer and without the companionship of my beloved wife. I'm tired, worn out by chemo, and miss her madly. And with all my friends gone, Earth holds no place for me anymore. My children all have lives of their own and we all know our stay here is not forever. As Blue Oyster Cult said, "Don't Fear the Reaper." So, it's no time to complain. It's time to reflect on all the precious moments that have graced this miraculous mystery called *Life* and take that next step. Life has been wondrous, breathtaking, and at times painfully cruel and unexpected, but I prefer to choose my own destiny, as I swallow a fistful of pills and gaze contentedly up at the mystical heavens, its ethereal light shining tantalizingly bright, warm, and feeling oh so right...all white, glorious white, as I slide peacefully into the eternal light of night.

THE RESURRECTION

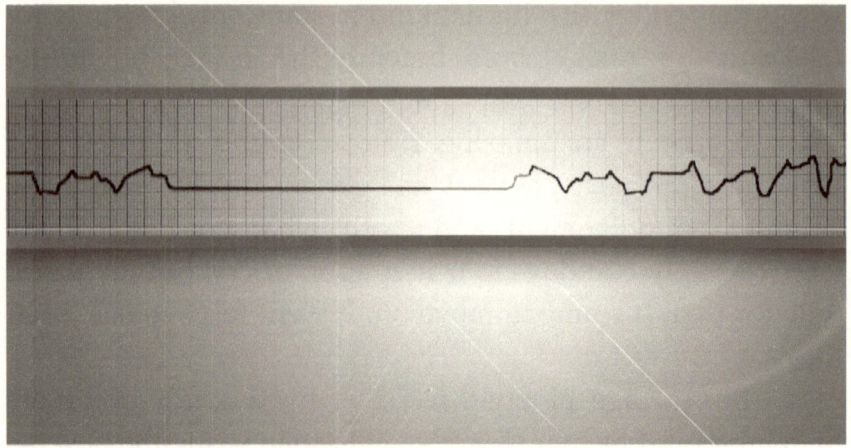

Sirens blared and lights flashed, as the gurney banged into the rear doors of the EMS truck. Unconscious, the gun-wounded victim was jettisoned out of the vehicle and pushed into the main entrance of the Emergency Room. EMS worker William Haley kept pressure on the gaping wound, while blood continued to gush out from the gauze pad, leaving a crimson trail down the pristine corridor. Police Officers Jim Lamont and Harry McCann followed close behind, but were stopped by Dr. Jason Stein.

"Hold on!" the doctor demanded. "I can't let you in, this man has lost a tremendous amount of blood and will surely die if I don't operate immediately." With that, Dr. Stein didn't wait for an answer and dashed into the Operating Room followed by four nurses.

Officer Lamont shook his rookie head and looked at his fifty-two-year-old partner. "Harry, did the bar owner give you any idea who this guy is?"

"No, just that he's a drifter. He never saw him before."

Jim rubbed his bristly chin. "Damn, it all happened so fast, I didn't even get a chance to check out his wallet."

Harry shrugged, used to the routine, and unwilling to give Jim too many details beyond the specific questions the greenhorn asked. As he walked toward the vending machine, he said, "Well, we'll know once they finish up with him in there." As he inserted a dollar bill into the machine, he added, "I'm sure we'll be here a while, Jimmy boy, so relax. As you saw, the guy's in really bad shape. He was beaten to a pulp *and* shot." He grabbed his Snickers bar and glanced at the OR doors. "Hell, they sure have their work cut out for them."

Jim paced back and forth, while Harry took a seat and continued to eat his chocolate bar. Jim was wired, this was his first real call to action, and he didn't like the odd events that occurred at El Coyote pub. He looked at Harry. "So, the bouncer at the bar said he saw the perp drag this guy out, into the alley, then beat the shit out of him. By the time he arrived, he saw the perp pull out a gun and shoot this poor bastard right in the chest, point blank range." Jim nervously rubbed his stubble again. "What do you make of that? And shouldn't we be trying to hunt down the gunman?"

Harry peeled back the wrapper further and eyed up the nutty Snickers bar, eager to get back to something he truly enjoyed. He was burnt out by the many years of seeing similar cases in the shitty part of Spanish Harlem he patrolled. After a while, one bloody body looked like another, and the human factor evaporated, leaving only bloody manikins being rushed to and fro in ambulances and into ERs. He rested the Snickers bar on his hefty thigh and looked up at his virile, young partner. "I called it in, Lamont. Jose and Miguel are on it." He raised his candy bar, and before biting, said, "They handle their kind better than we can. So, chill out and relax."

Jim squinted. "What do you mean *they handle their kind better*?" Irritably, Jim walked in front of Harry and peered down, straight into his blue eyes. "What kind of racist bullshit is that?"

Harry gazed up, annoyed. He was pissed that he had to swallow quickly, without savoring the chocolaty flavor, not to mention the gritty nuts that he loved so much. "Don't hand me that racist crap, Junior," he said while licking his brown lips. "When you work this beat long enough, you'll see that what I said is just the plain ugly truth. Latino thugs don't appreciate white cops, nor do black crooks like white cops, and so on. It's always best to put the same race in each community. It keeps the peace."

Jim scoffed, "Jesus, you don't even realize what comes out of your racist mouth, do you?"

Harry rolled his eyes. "Jimmy, what you don't understand is that most often we're not dealing with enlightened people in these poverty-infested slums. The criminal minds that we confront don't share your or my views of equality and tolerance. It's sad, but it's just the plain truth. And the white cops who truly are racist and beat up black or Latino criminals have only inflamed race relations. If black or Latino cops beat on their own kind it wouldn't stir the media into a frenzy and get everyone hyper sensitive and riled about race relations. So that's why I'm an advocate for quenching racial issues in criminal cases by having Latino cops deal with Latino thugs."

Jim shook his head. "That's ludicrous, Harry. So, segregation is your answer to improving race relations, is that it?"

"If you haven't noticed, newbie doobie, urban cities are segregated already: Little Italy, Chinatown, Harlem, Spanish Harlem, Williamsburg, and so on. So, yeah, segregation in urban areas sounds about right, Jim."

"No, it sounds like you need to retire, Harry."

As Harry bristled, Dr. Stein approached them, his shoulders rounded, his face gaunt. As Jim and Harry gazed his way, the doctor uttered. "I'm sorry to say, the patient died. The poor fella didn't have much of a chance, he bled out."

Harry stood up. "Well, you did what you could." He looked at Jim. "I guess that wraps it up for us."

Jim huffed. "Speak for yourself, Harry. I need to find out what the poor man's name was. I'm sure his family would like to know."

Harry rolled his eyes, as Dr. Stein said, "Actually, I'm going to do something quite unconventional."

Harry and Jim peered at the doctor, curious, as he continued, "I plan on trying an EPR."

Now Harry and Jim were even more baffled, as Harry said, "The man's *dead*, Doctor. So, what the hell is an EPR?"

"It's a very new procedure, and quite revolutionary," Dr. Stein said. "EPR stands for Emergency Preservation and Resuscitation."

Harry squinted. "But didn't you already try to resuscitate him?"

The doctor smiled. "Yes, but only with the archaic tools at our disposal; namely, defibrillator pads. But the patient's heart could not possibly restart without blood, Officer McCann."

"Okay, now I'm really lost," Harry said. "Just what the hell are you proposing?"

As a nurse approached, the doctor instructed, "Please prepare for an EPR." As the nurse's eyes widened, he added, "Quickly!"

The nurse darted back into the Operating Room, as Dr. Stein turned back toward the police officers. "The process entails injecting ice-cold saline into the patient's empty bloodstream, which immediately chills the entire body down to 50 degrees Fahrenheit, and actually stops brain activity. Basically, it's suspended animation, but only for a brief amount of time."

Jim was flabbergasted. "That's awesome!"

Harry shook his head. "Wait a minute. Why would you waste your time resurrecting a drifter like this? If it was Steve Jobs or someone like that, sure, but this deadbeat was beat up and shot. I'm sure he's a no-good thug."

Dr. Stein smirked. "Officer, I took a Hippocratic oath to serve and protect the lives of every patient that comes into my hands. Now, *I must go!* I only have a two-hour window to resuscitate this man!" With that, the doctor raced back into the OR.

Jim glared at his partner. "And who are *you* to play God, Harry?"

Harry snorted. "Jesus Christ! You young millennials never quit, do ya? If you had been quick enough to ascertain the low down on this deadbeat, you'd know he was an illegal drifter from South America. I talked to Rosita, the barmaid. She told me this guy gave her the creeps and she overheard him arguing with the guy who pummeled him and then shot him. It was all in Spanish, naturally, but evidently the gunman said this guy killed his twelve-year-old daughter."

Jim's eyes widened as he gritted his teeth. "Why the hell didn't you tell me that!?" he blasted.

Harry rolled his eyes. "Because, like I told you, I instructed Jose and Miguel to follow up on my leads. They'll call me when they get additional information. I'm too old for this crap and I don't have the time or patience to hold your hand and walk you through this." Harry sighed, exasperated. "The bottom line is, this guy is a piece of shit, and doesn't deserve being brought back from the dead."

Jim's mouth and lips twisted as if he ate a rotten egg. He was beyond pissed. "I just love how you play God with a man's life, a man who you have it on the word of a single barmaid that he's a criminal, and also decide that *I'm* not worthy of your precious time." Jim had all to do to keep from clocking Harry, as he seethed, "If I weren't a cop, I'd—"

"Do what? Punch me?" Harry interjected. As Jim snarled, Harry went on, "If you're so pissed, get a transfer. I don't have time for this shit. I retire in four months."

"Indeed you should!" Jim spat.

Just then, Harry's cell phone rang. As he answered the call, Dr. Stein approached them, a grin spread across his face. "Great news, gentlemen! It was a resounding success. You're both witnesses to a milestone in medical history."

Jim's face beamed. "That's fantastic! Can I speak with him?"

"Certainly, he's made an astounding recovery." The doctor raised his finger. "But please, make it short. He needs rest."

Harry ended his call, and looked at the doctor. "Well, I hope you're happy, Doctor. Because I just found out that the man you resurrected is Pedro Lopez."

Jim interjected, "Oh, so you're pissed that he saved an illegal Latino's life?"

Again, Harry rolled his eyes, and continued, "No, Junior. Pedro Lopez just so happens to be one of the deadliest serial killers in history. He raped and murdered over three hundred and fifty children in Columbia, Ecuador, and Peru. Most were young, innocent girls. Lopez served twenty years in solitary confinement in Ecuador, but was paroled. He hasn't been seen since." As the doctor and Jim's faces blanched, Harry added, "Well, not until he appeared in our backyard, that is." He looked at the doctor. "And *you*, Dr. Stein, brought him back to life."

Just then, three nurses ran out of the OR screaming, hysterical. "He killed nurse Peterson!"

Harry and Jim dashed into the OR with guns drawn, only to see the dead nurse on the ground—Pedro Lopez was gone. They spun around as the three nurses reentered the OR. The head nurse explained that after killing nurse Peterson Lopez darted out the rear door.

Officer Jim took off after him while Harry rubbed his temples.

Dr. Stein reentered the OR, his face marred with remorse. "I'm so sorry. I had no idea."

Harry shook his head. "I got chewed out by my partner for wanting to play God, just for preferring that this deadbeat remained dead. Yet, *you* were the one who actually played God, Dr. Stein. Your medical science can indeed produce wonders, but how and on whom its used is where your Hippocratic oath fails miserably. Idealism must confront realism to be truly beneficial."

Just then, Jim returned, out of breath and sweating. "He's gone, all right. I looked everywhere."

"That's just swell," Harry moaned. "We now have a psychopathic serial killer on the loose, one the Latinos call the *Monster of the Andes*."

Harry gazed disparagingly at Dr. Stein, "And *you* brought the monster back to life. Outstanding work, Dr. *Franken*–Stein."

~ *The End* ~

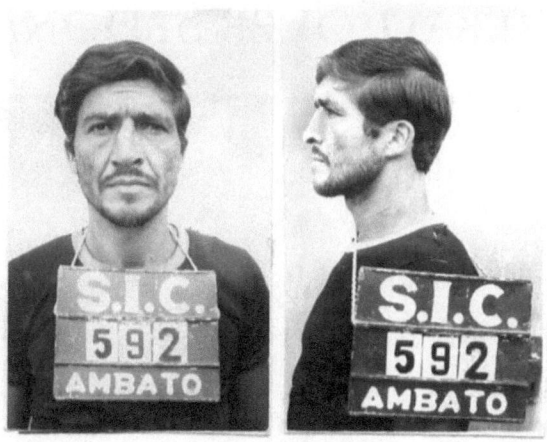

[This chilling tale presents one speculative scenario of what could possibly happen. Pedro Lopez is in fact one of the deadliest serial killers in history. He raped and killed over 350 children, most young girls. As mentioned herein, his killing spree was primarily in Columbia, Ecuador, and Peru, and Pedro was given the nickname *Monster of the Andes*. He served 20 years in prison, but was released. His whereabouts are still unknown. Additionally, the EPR medical procedure is currently under development and expected to be perfected sometime in 2020. Those pronounced dead, could possibly be resurrected. An amazing procedure indeed, but one that would require careful and logical guidelines.]

A FIREBALL OVER SEDONA

The fireball streaked through the Arizona night sky at high velocity as three hikers on Chicken Point Overlook in Sedona gasped.

Angela looked at her fiancé. "Billy, what the hell is that!?" she exclaimed wide-eyed and shaken.

Billy couldn't take his eyes off the unidentified object. "Beats me."

Their third-wheel, Joey, said, "Looks like a meteor or a comet."

Just then, the blazing light appeared to stop, then exploded in mid-air, at what appeared to be a mile or so above the barren terrain in the distance.

As they each blinked, Billy started to run back toward his Jeep. "Come on! Let's go to check it out."

With that, Angela and Joey followed suit, dashing through the darkness and hopping into Billy's Jeep Cherokee. As they each peeled off their backpacks, Billy slammed the manual shift into gear and started to race off in the Southeast direction of the explosion. As they bounced around inside the vehicle, barreling over the hilly terrain, a mule deer ran across their path, almost colliding into the front fender. Billy swerved. Riding briefly on two wheels, the Jeep wobbled, then regained its footing as it continued onward. Meanwhile, they each looked at each other and sighed with relief.

Joey strained his eyes to look into the dark distance. "I'm telling you, it must have been a meteor or a comet."

Angela shook her head. "No way, Joey. Didn't you see how it stopped in mid-air, then exploded? I think it was a UFO, and it malfunctioned or was shot down. Or perhaps it was something from Area 51. Roswell isn't that far away."

"I don't believe in that UFO nonsense," Joey said, "That moment of delay must have been a visual distortion," he said. "The sharp angle it descended from the sky gives all indications that it was on a crash course. And I'll bet a million dollars that when we get to the crash site, we'll either see a crater by a meteor, or no crater at all, proving it was a comet."

Angela squinted, confused, as Joey explained, "It's like the Tunguska event in Russia, back in 1908. The trees were all blown down in a radial burst around the point of impact, yet no crater exists. That's because the ice of the comet vaporized before hitting Earth. Yet its shockwave blew over everything around it, as if an Atomic blast."

Angela shook her head. "Joey, in this day and age, for people not to believe that there are other intelligent life forms out there is just plain stupid, or a pathetic sign of megalomania, to think we humans are the only intelligent beings in the universe."

As Billy swerved around a cactus plant, he chimed in, "Well, I'm all for believing there's life out there somewhere in the universe, Angela, but I don't believe any intelligent beings visited us in the past or present, at least not yet."

Angela looked at her fiancé with a touch of surprise. "Billy, you must be kidding? We used to have conversations about Erich von Däniken's *Chariots of the Gods?* and the Egyptian pyramids. You agreed that it baffled you."

As Billy tried to maintain control of the Jeep as it bounced over rocky mounds and crushed small plants, he glanced at Angela sitting in the passenger's seat. "Sweetheart, yes, I did at one time give credence to some other explanation, but that was almost a decade ago. Upon further thought, however, it would have been ludicrous for an advanced species to come here only to teach humans how to build a pyramid out of carved stone. Why not steel, titanium, or some unknown superior element?"

Angela felt betrayed. "Why didn't you tell me this before? I can't believe this!"

Billy smiled, almost condescendingly. "And I can't believe that *you* still believe aliens built the pyramids."

Angela shook her head, peeved. "Those blocks of stone were carved almost perfectly, and those towering structures were built without modern power tools or cranes. You know that, yet how can you explain their construction using only crude human ingenuity?"

Billy slowed down, keeping his eyes on the dark terrain, and replied, "Angela, people, in general, under estimate the brilliance of human ingenuity. It's a glaring fact that only a handful of savants and their underlings or competitors create the mindboggling advances in human society. Only one man developed the Tesla Coil—Nikola Tesla. Tesla's long list of inventions was also hatched from his brain, working in solitude. Yes, he observed the work of others, and read up on new developments, but when it came down to invention, he avoided distractions and worked alone. The billions that constitute the masses are not the brain-stormers, or the movers and shakers. *No!* They're the idle reapers of the savants' kinetic ingenuity. Only one man, Einstein, came up with the Theory of Relativity. His followers, perhaps a few hundred at most, utilized his brain exercise to develop Atomic energy. So, the Pharaoh's engineer, or engineers, developed methods to create the pyramids, which thousands of slave laborers were instructed to carry out. Besides, why would a superior alien race help a self-centered, arrogant Pharaoh to create a tomb to glorify and deify himself?"

As Angela's face wilted, never giving such thoughts much consideration, Billy added, "I'm sorry, sweetheart, it's childish to think otherwise. If you were to travel to a distant planet where lower life forms thrived, yet were oppressed and ruled by one self-loving dolt, would you help him to create a tomb just to covet all the wealth and jewels of his greedy reign? And mind you, build it with archaic stones, rather than materials your advanced race is accustomed to working with?"

Just then, Joey yelled, "Look out!"

Billy's eyes widened as he cut the wheel, nearly crashing into an alien, whose four arms rose up defensively. Its two large eyes squinted at the bright headlights, while the Jeep came to an abrupt stop several yards away. The trio's heads all snapped back, as they gazed at the odd creature, standing eight-feet tall and now dimly lit by the Jeep's red taillights.

"Oh God!" Joey yelped, while Angela whispered, "Shh! It will hear you."

Billy just stared in shock, as he uttered. "Too late for that, it can see us."

The alien's large head swung around and looked at the vehicle. Its head tilted, evidently trying to size up the odd metallic object with red lights. It started to walk toward the Jeep with a noticeable limp.

"It's hurt," Joey said.

"I don't give a crap," Angela blurted, "Let's get out of here!"

Billy turned around and threw the Jeep into first gear. "Peering in the rearview mirror, he said, "I'm with you, sweetheart!"

With that, Billy punched the accelerator as the Jeep lunged forward.

Meanwhile, Joey and Angela's eyes were glued on the creature, which now started to run with a limp after them.

Billy power-shifted, getting the vehicle up to seventy-five miles an hour, as the alien was left behind in a wake of dry dust. Driving over the hilly, desert-like terrain, Billy turned onto the dirt path of Chapel Trail and tore up the hill, eventually coming onto the pavement of Chapel Rd. He downshifted, and drove up the mountain road and came to an abrupt stop at the Chapel of the Holy Cross.

The impressive chapel was commissioned by the sculptor Marguerite Staude (a student of Frank Lloyd Wright's), and designed by the architects Richard Hein and August K. Strotz.

Angela looked at Billy and squinted. "Why did you come here? We should go into town and alert the authorities."

"Let's just take sanctuary here until daylight," Billy said. He looked up at the Chapel, a little marvel of human ingenuity that was built into the mountainside. The site was magnificent, and as Billy now came to believe, *if* there were an all-powerful God, this would surely be a place he'd call home and watch over.

Meanwhile, Joey quickly added, "I'm with Billy. I'm sure that creature won't follow us here, Angela. It's hurt and will probably search the houses in the valley first."

Angela looked at both of them. "We can't stay here and let that monster harm anyone down below." She looked at Billy. "Well? Come on. We must do something!"

Billy pulled out his cell phone. "I got it covered," he said as he dialed 9-1-1. A woman receptionist answered, as Billy gushed, "I'd like to report a UFO, *and* an alien creature!"

The woman's voice queried, "Say that again?"

Billy reiterated, and the woman whined, "It's way too late for prank phone calls, sonny. I'm in no mood for horseplay. Do you hear me!?"

"And do you hear *me*!" Billy shouted. "I'm *not* fooling around. We saw a spacecraft crash into the desert near Chicken Point Overlook. We drove out toward the crash site, only to come face-to-face with an alien, which we almost hit. It was clearly injured and chased after us, but I left it in the dust. We're currently at the Chapel of the Holy Cross. *Now*, can you get the police here *immediately!*?"

The receptionist was silent for but a moment, then said, "Jesus Christ! We just received another call about a UFO in the same vicinity."

"No shit!" Billy said. "Get the police here ASAP!"

"Will do!" the woman said, "Hang in there, and *wait*. Don't do anything foolish!"

"Foolish!? Why do you think I called *you*!" Billy said, and hung up.

He looked at Joey then Angela. "The police are on their way. Let's just stay put. Besides, we have a good vantage point from up here. He dug into his backpack and pulled out his infrared night binoculars. "Come on!" he said, as he ran to the edge of the Chapel's platform. Swiftly, he peered out over the solid stone railing, into the blackness of night down below.

Joey eagerly grabbed his wrist. "Let me see!"

Billy yanked his arm away. "Chill out!" he said peevishly. "Let me see if I can spot the damn thing first."

Angela paced to and fro, then finally walked up beside Billy and said, "So, you were just saying you don't believe in UFOs. Now what do you think, Mr. *Doubt*-fire?"

Billy took his head away from the binoculars and peered at her. "Angela, I said I didn't believe we were visited by intelligent beings in the past or present, at least not yet." He looked back into the infrared binoculars, and added, "But evidently, *yet* has finally arrived!"

Angela frowned. "Actually, that doesn't make me feel any better." Worriedly, she peered out into the darkness, trying to see if she could spot the alien herself. As she squinted, Billy blurted, "Holy cow! I see it!"

Joey and Angela rushed by his side, each trying to pull the binoculars out of his hand in opposite directions. Counteracting their efforts, the binoculars only jostled slightly, while Billy elbowed each of them. "Hands off, you imbeciles! You'll make me lose sight of it."

"Okay! Mr. Greedy," Joey whined. "Hog it all to yourself."

Billy huffed as he continued to track the limping alien. "Grow up, you idiot! This is a landmark event in human history, and you're going to blow our chances to track this creature down, so when the cops arrive we can direct them accordingly."

Angela nodded as she looked at Joey. "I hate to agree, but he's right."

Billy shook his head, and glanced briefly at his fiancée. "What's with the animosity? Because I disagreed about the pyramids being built by aliens?"

"It's more than that, Billy. This goes beyond a simple disagreement, this goes to humankind's most critical belief systems: The belief in one God verses a whole new paradigm, a system where alien biological life forms visited this planet in the past, and by doing so obliterated the archaic tenants of all known religions, none of which ever mentioned life on other planets. They all ignorantly said our planet and we humans were the center of the universe, the ones made in God's image. It's all bunk! And this alien proves it."

"Well, that proof is making its way up here," Billy said nervously. He lowered the binoculars and pointed at the base of the spiral walkway that led up to the mountain Chapel. "It's limping its way up the ramp."

"Holy shit!" Joey squealed as fear gripped him tight. "What do we do now?"

Billy handed Joey the binoculars. "I don't know about you, but I'm going into the Chapel to pray."

Angela smirked. *"Pray!"* Seriously? That's your solution?"

As Billy kept walking toward the Chapel, Joey said, "Yeah, what the hell are you doing, Billy? This four-armed monster is crawling up here to probably slash us to shreds and eat us, and all you can do is sit and pray?"

Billy kept walking and said, "I doubt an intelligent being that crafted a spaceship to travel through the galaxy wants to kill and eat us, Joey. I'm no holy roller, but perhaps, just perhaps, it understands the meaning of humility." He stopped and looked back. "Even if we have no clue about God or the Creator, or whatever form it takes, we should at least show it that we're humble enough to admit we don't have all the answers and aren't arrogant enough to profess we do. That, I believe, is a good start."

With that, Billy walked into the Chapel and knelt before the huge cross, which eerily overlooked the valley of darkness.

Behind him, outside, he suddenly heard a jarring commotion, as Angela and Joey's screams echoed throughout the valley, while gunshots rang out. Billy leapt to his feet and dashed outside, only to come upon four police officers with smoking guns, while Joey and Angela gazed down at the wriggling creature on the ground.

As brown liquid oozed out of its body, the creature moaned with the heart-wrenching wail of a dying seal. The police shined their flashlights on the alien, as Billy walked closer, gritting his teeth. He looked at the police. "What happened? Did the alien make any threatening maneuvers?"

Angela stepped beside Billy. "It was heading toward me, Billy. I don't know what it intended, but I screamed. Before I knew it, the police opened fire."

Officer Henry Johnson stepped forward. "That's right. This hideous monster was making an advance toward her, we had no option but to protect her."

Angela looked at Billy annoyed. "That's more than what *you* did! Running away into the Chapel like that."

Billy bit his lip. "Angela, like the faulty hypothesis of the alien architects of the pyramids, I had some time to reevaluate my initial fear of this creature. I truly believe it didn't come all the way here to slaughter us."

"Oh, do you," Angela said smugly. "That's easy for you to say, being inside the Chapel and not out here with this ugly creature plodding toward me."

Just then, the alien moaned and lifted one of its four arms, which it slipped into one of its pouches. The police immediately pointed their guns at the dying creature, as Billy yelled, "Stop! Hold on. It's not reaching for a weapon."

As the police wavered in their decisions, the alien pulled out a gold-anodized aluminum plaque. Billy's eyes widened with shock as his heart twisted with remorse. He instantly recognized the famous plaque.

At Carl Sagan's request, it was placed on the Pioneer 10 space probe. Having been launched in 1972, the probe flew to Jupiter, then was the first spacecraft to fly out of the solar system into deep space. Sagan's hopes were that the plaque—which featured a naked male and female with symbols indicating Earth's location—would give alien life forms a friendly clue about human life and the ship's origin.

With a final breath and a choke, the alien whimpered, as its hand fell, the plaque of friendship in its dead hand.

"Shit!" Billy cried. "What a fine greeting we gave this space traveler!" He looked at Angela, then at the police. "So, tell me, who really *are* the monsters?"

BABY GIRL

The first time I laid eyes on my darling little baby girl, I wasn't sure what to expect. I had grown up in a family of all boys, and she seemed so small and frail. But as the months and years rolled by, she had blossomed into a shapely and magnificent young girl.

Her adorable little face with big magnetic eyes radiated her inner tenderness and charm and easily captured one's heart. It was a magnificent part of her DNA. In a word, she was *irresistible*: so much so, that family and friends could readily feel the warmth of her affectionate personality. Even as she grew older she maintained her alluring purity and innocence: most rare. She truly was one of God's masterful creations.

That might sound like the biased ravings of a proud parent, but my darling little girl affected others in a similar fashion, never once had I heard otherwise.

As I'd come home from work, she would always, without fail, greet me with an adorable expression on her face. Or would sit at the piano or window: just waiting to greet me and say hello in her soft, loving way.

Many times, while I lost myself in work at the computer, I would feel a tender tap on my back, summoning me, reminding me, that it was time to take a break: it was playtime. I would get up and have a catch with her or just engage in other activities that usually ended with warm loving embraces and a tender kiss on her head. Those precious moments were as much for me as they were for her, her need for love, as *love* is what she was.

But as the years rolled by, arthritis set in. It was much too soon for a young girl. The pain of watching her limp and struggle, with an occasional whimper, cut me like a knife, yet it was only the beginning of a downward spiral, as blood work and tests were taken and my darling girl began losing weight. Her once youthful playfulness was now mired in pain, but pain that she bore stoically with great dignity. She was too sweet and considerate to bother others with her agony, which after another round of tests and X-rays indicated that she had cancer and fluid in her lungs. The prognosis was a deathblow.

No parent should ever outlive their young ones, yet life does not play by the storybook notion of "they all lived happily ever after." The brutal and punishing reality was that we had to watch my baby girl decline, day after day, week after week, until she stopped eating for days on end: her breathing terribly labored.

No more did she greet me when I came home from work.

No more did she sneak up behind me and tap my back to play.

No more did she even have the energy or desire for our routine embraces and tender moments, as she shied away from life, seeking solitude so that she may suffer in silence and not disturb the rest of the family.

She had deteriorated to the point that the simple task of breathing was a laborious chore, as only one-sixth of her lungs were operational, while her cancerous tumors maliciously grew, further stripping this once glowing and tender bundle of innocence and joy to a mere shell of tissue and bones.

With the doctor suggesting euthanasia, the hardest decision in my life was contemplated, then painfully made. The last embrace and kisses no longer contained the joyful radiance and bliss of days past, but instead were like burning needles to the heart, as tears filled my eyes and cascaded down my face. It was a horrible, horrible day: a disturbing solar eclipse that blackened my world.

The irreplaceable void that plagues my days will eventually pass, so people say, but my darling little baby girl will always have a special place in my heart, as she was the best cat a man could ever have, and a truly magnificent little being.

Thank You

To all the great sources of inspiration, from novelists to nonfiction and from all the other sources of media to life experiences, that have fed my imagination, I am most grateful, as the art of creation and speculation cannot be spawned in a vacuum.

To my dear wife Eileen, who has enriched my life immeasurably, and was honored in *Tales of the Heart*, I love you! To my steadfast family, and friends who have supported my creative endeavors and my editors, marketers and to all the international contest judges who have voted several of my books as award winners, I am truly grateful. *Thank you!*

— Rich DiSilvio

My Nazi Nemesis

GOLD AWARD WINNER

★★★★★ "DiSilvio's plot is cunning and ingenious!"
-- *Jack Magnus for Readers' Favorite*

A deadly love triangle launches a father and daughter team to hunt down a nefarious Nazi. Yet twists and turns abound, leading to a shocking climax.

Hardcover: 9780981762586
Paperback: 9780981762579
eBook: 9780981762593

A Blazing Gilded Age

INTERNATIONAL AWARD WINNER

A riveting rags-to-riches saga about a poor family's struggle to survive amid a nation burning with ambition yet bleeding with injustice. Features, Teddy Roosevelt, JP Morgan, Mark Twain, Tesla and more.

Lauded by HISTORY/A+E and noted biographer Roger DiSilvestro.

Hardcover: 9780981762562
Paperback: 9780981762555
eBook: 9780997680720

Tales of Titans Series

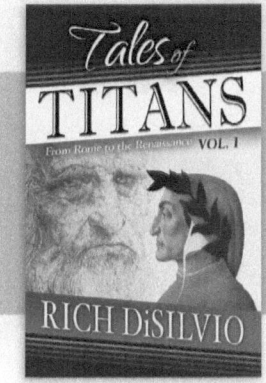

Tales of Titans brings great historical figures to life with concise yet compelling essays, coupled with engaging narratives that enlighten readers to their miraculous deeds, and misdeeds, that have significantly shaped Western civilization.

This handsomely illustrated series offers readers brief biographical overviews and cogent analysis, while the quasi-fictional scenarios transport readers into a fascinating past, whereby putting flesh on the bones of several titans and offering glimpses into their hearts, minds, and actions.
.
Tales of Titans, Vol. I : From Rome to the Renaissance
Augustus & Livia, Vespasian & Titus, Hadrian, Constantine, Dante, Brunelleschi, Columbus, Vespucci, King Ferdinand, Pope Alexander VI & Cesare Borgia, and Leonardo da Vinci.

Tales of Titans, Vol. II: Renaissance to the Electro/Atomic Age
The Medicis, Gutenberg, Lorenzo de Medici, Savonarola, Leonardo & Machiavelli, Martin Luther, Queen Elizabeth I, Shakespeare, Galileo, Darwin, Marx, Stalin, Freud, Marconi, Edison, Tesla, Westinghouse, Einstein, Fermi and von Braun.

Tales of Titans, Vol. III: Founding Fathers, Women Warriors & WWII
Samuel Adams, Thomas Paine, George Washington, John Adams, Thomas Jefferson, James Madison, Alexander Hamilton, Ben Franklin, Sybil Ludington, James Armistead Lafayette, Elizabeth Cady Stanton, Susan B. Anthony, Harriet Tubman, Adolf Hitler, FDR & Churchill

Liszt's *Dante Symphony*

A historical mystery/thriller highlighting the belligerent rise of Nazi Germany from its Prussian roots, replete with ciphers, spies, murder and a stellar cast, including Albert Einstein, Rossini, Liszt, Nazi officers and Adolf Hitler.

Hardcover: 9780981762548
Paperback: 9780981762531
eBook: 9780997680713

The Winds of Time

The Winds of Time is a historical tour de force of Western civilization by Rich DiSilvio.

With masterful style, DiSilvio paints a fascinating historical canvas with the flare of a consummate artist. Key figures and the primary cultures that literally shaped the Western world are candidly analyzed, revealing both the dark and luminous sides of mankind. Moreover, DiSilvio's insightful essays add intriguing new dimensions to the historical record.

Hardcover: 9780981762524
eBook: 9780997680706

SILVER MEDAL WINNER
Meet My Famous Friends

Inspiring kids with Humor!
A whimsical picture book that pays homage to great historical figures in imaginative ways.

Author/Illustrator Rich DiSilvio presents a broad array of geniuses and heroes in a humorous and compelling fashion by altering their names and appearances, whereby making us see very familiar people in very different ways.

While children will get a kick out of looking at the comical artwork, teens and even adults will appreciate the witty play on words, inventive creations, and perhaps glean a thing or two about some of these iconic people who had a great influence on society in one form or another. Their lives and contributions have uplifted humanity in various ways, thus being great role models for young and old alike.

Hardcover: 9780997680751   Paperback: 9780997680768   eBook: 9780997680775

PURPLE DRAGONFLY WINNER
Danny and the DreamWeaver

A MS novelette by Mark Poe (aka Rich DiSilvio) about the power of dreams and the imagination.

When Danny meets Nostrildamus in his dream a bizarre journey begins!

Packed with dry humor, a mystery, and zany-looking artists, like Michelanjello & Hippopotamus Bosch, *Danny and the DreamWeaver* is an imaginative adventure of criminal intrigue and art history that demonstrates the importance of looking at life differently.

Paperback: 9780997680737
eBook: 9780997680744

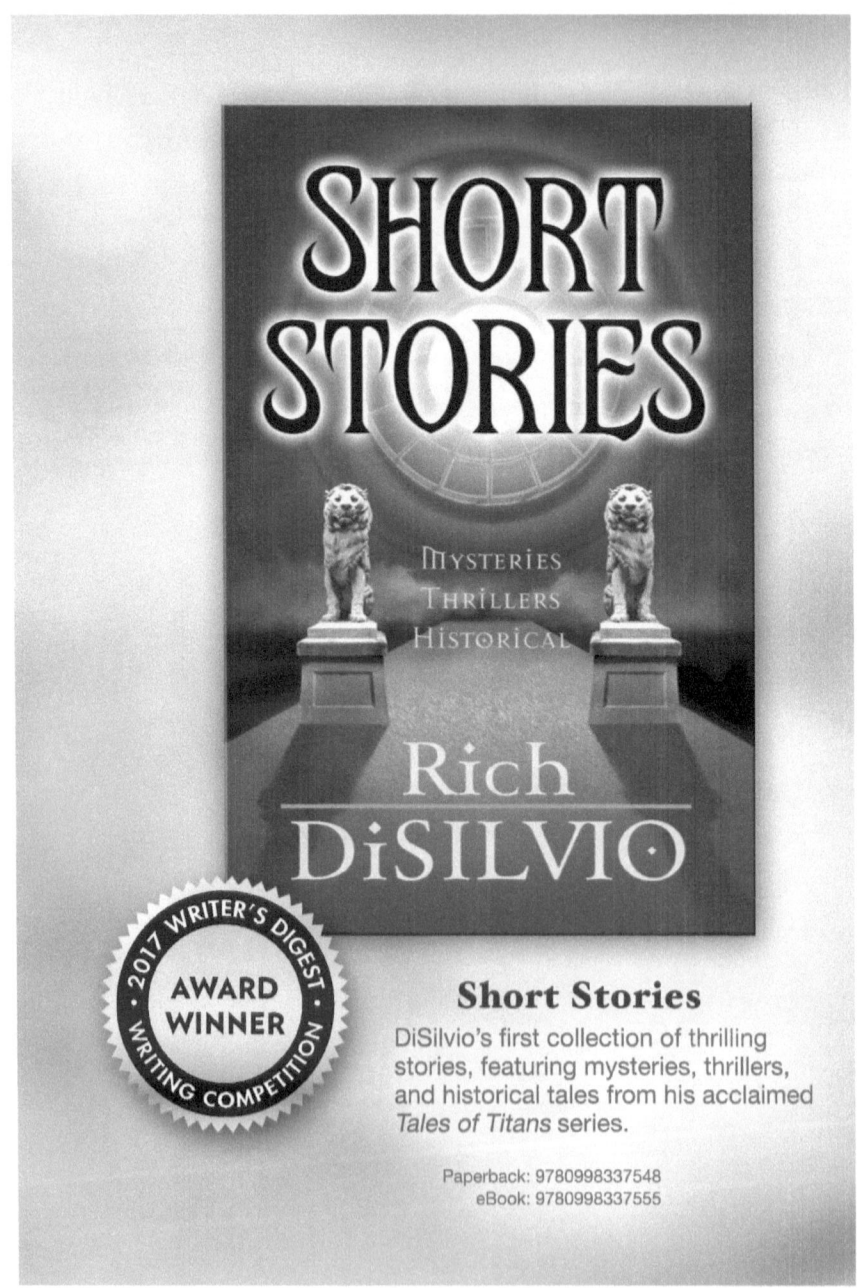

Short Stories

DiSilvio's first collection of thrilling stories, featuring mysteries, thrillers, and historical tales from his acclaimed *Tales of Titans* series.

Paperback: 9780998337548
eBook: 9780998337555

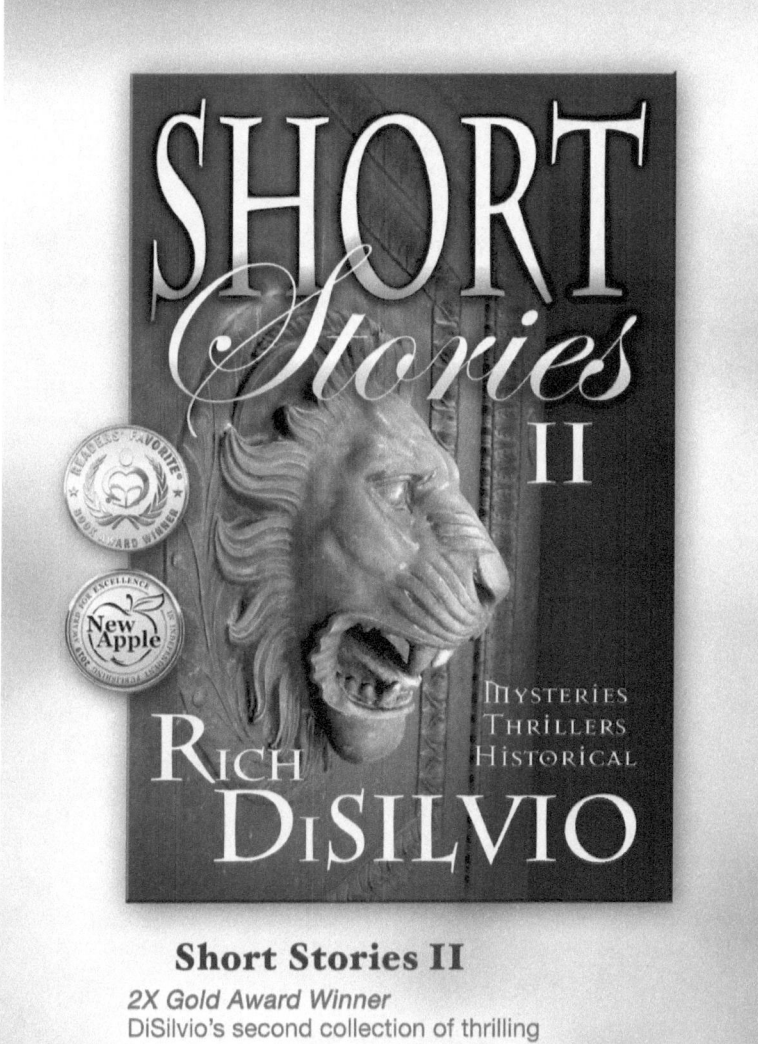

Short Stories II

2X Gold Award Winner
DiSilvio's second collection of thrilling
stories, featuring mysteries, thrillers,
and historical tales from his acclaimed
Tales of Titans series.

Paperback: 9780998337562
eBook: 9780998337579

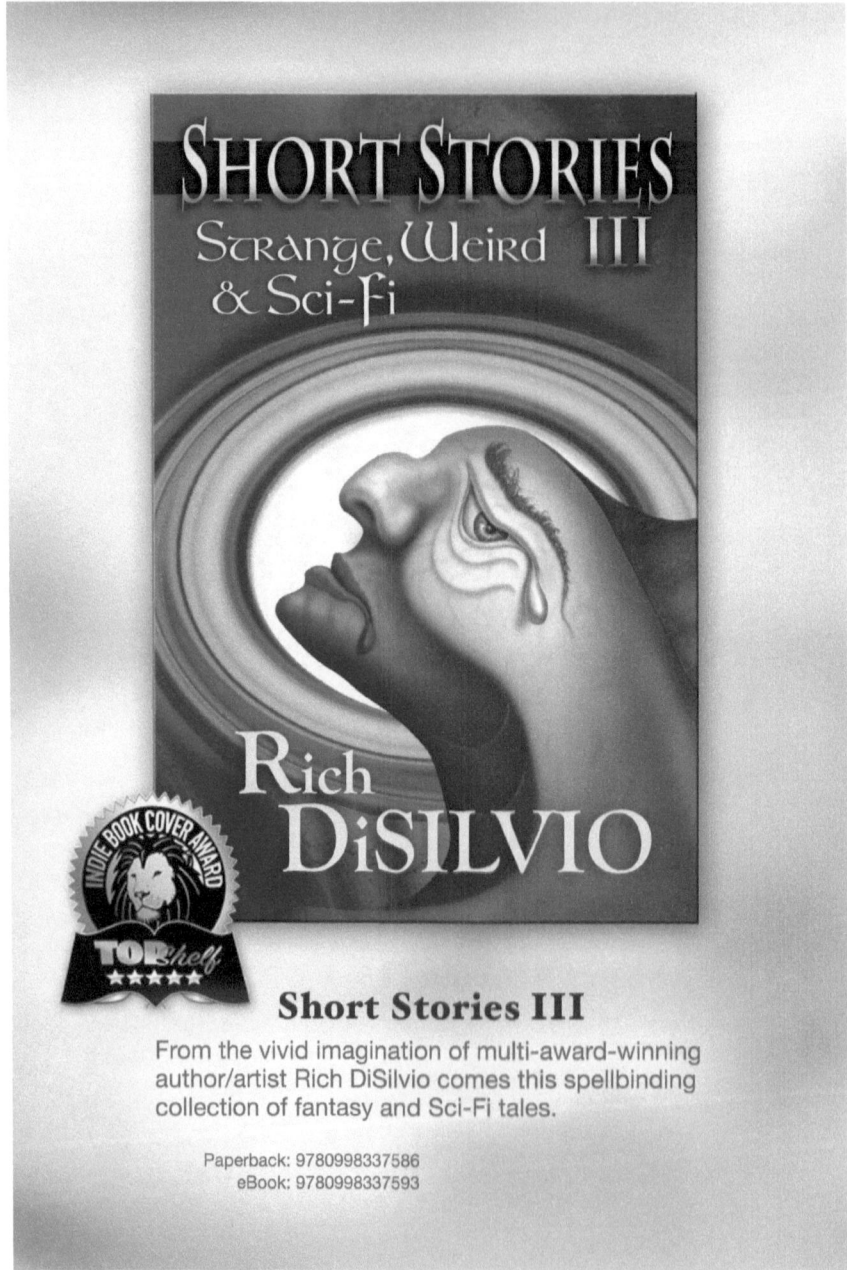

Short Stories III

From the vivid imagination of multi-award-winning author/artist Rich DiSilvio comes this spellbinding collection of fantasy and Sci-Fi tales.

Paperback: 9780998337586
eBook: 9780998337593

Short Stories IV

From the vivid imagination of multi-award-winning author/artist Rich DiSilvio comes this spellbinding second collection of fantasy and Sci-Fi tales.

Paperback: 9781950052004
eBook: 9781950052011

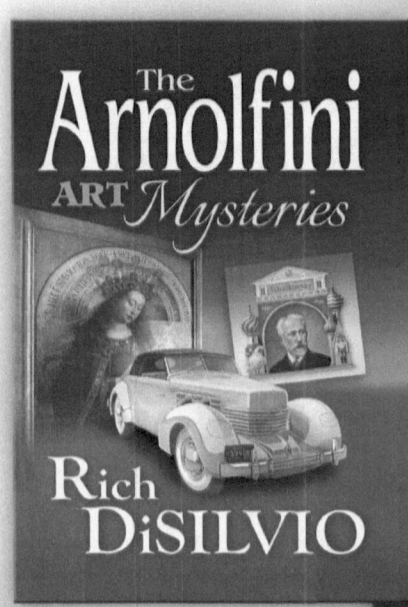

The Arnolfini Art Mysteries

The debut collection of riveting mysteries, featuring the clever and dapper P.I. Armand Arnolfini, as he hunts down crafty forgers, unscrupulous thieves and even ruthless killers to save famous works of art from oblivion.

Hardcover: 978-1-950052-04-2
Paperback: 978-1-950052-02-8
eBook: 978-1-950052-03-5

Arnolfini Art Mysteries 2

Armand is back, this time with his new wife Andrea to solve a string of art crimes. The duo hunt down Leonardo's lost *Lead and the Swan*, and an unknown masterwork by the Baroque female master Artemisia Gentileschi.

Paperback: 978-1-950052-06-6
eBook: 978-1-950052-05-9

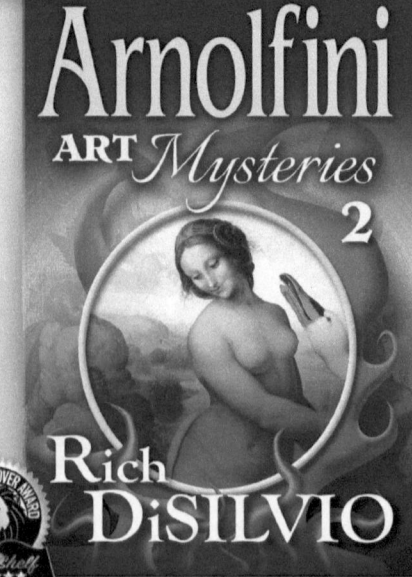

Special Note to the Reader

This compilation is a hodgepodge of thoughts infused into a few short stories and several narrations, the latter perhaps striking the reader as odd, and certainly unconventional, yet all fall under the banner of Speculative Musings and do offer perspectives worthy of contemplation.

This collection also offers more dystopian tales than usual, being a phase of reflection due to social, political, and technological reasons. Some of those dire issues deserve our attention with the hopes that humankind will take the warning signs seriously and commit themselves to ensuring that some of these bleak outcomes never come to be.

This collection even includes a dark poetic tale in rhyme with touches of humor. Other tales are reflections of the mystery of life and death, for the older we become the inevitability of the *next world*, or simply *the end*, becomes more prevalent and real. But, also infused in these narrations are recollections of the sheer beauties of life and the magical power of love and creation. I've even included a eulogy to my dear cat, Nugget. May she rest in peace.

For those sampling my works for the first time, I suggest you try other editions in this series before passing judgment, as I know this collection contains works that are unconventional and may not be understood or enjoyed by the common reader. For those acquainted with my works, they know I like to push the envelope and explore new horizons. But, all in all, I hope everyone can walk away with something profound to truly think about, and can be entertained by the more conventional moments within. Thank you for reading this collection.

It would be greatly appreciated if you take a moment to post a brief review about this book on your favorite retailer's website or social media forum.